SAM McBRATNEY

Sam McBratney is a versatile and award-winning author, best known for his best-selling picture book, *Guess How Much I Love You*. Sam, who lives in Northern Ireland, used to be a teacher but now writes full-time. *You Just Don't Listen!*, originally published as *Put a Saddle on the Pig*, won the Irish Children's Book Association's Bisto Award.

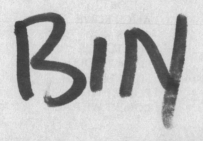

Also in the **Contents** series

Contents

Sam McBratney

Funny, how the magic starts...

Mammoth

First published in Great Britain 1989
by Methuen Children's Books Ltd
Published 1990 by Mammoth
Reissued 1999 by Mammoth
an imprint of Egmont Children's Books Limited
239 Kensington High Street, London W8 6SA

ISBN 0 7497 0313 X

1 3 5 7 9 10 8 6 4 2

A CIP catalogue record for this title
is available at the British Library

Printed in Great Britain
by Cox and Wyman Ltd., Reading, Berkshire

PART

1

Chapter

1

'Monica – I think it would be nice if you made friends with that new boy across the road.'

I glared at my dear mother's back as she peeped through the slats of our living-room blind like a born spy. Making friends is a personal thing. I have my own life to lead, after all.

'I'm doing my English homework right now, Mummy. It's quite complicated.'

'Well I said you would, Monica. I was talking to his mother down at the shops and she said he was feeling a bit lonely. Of course I said you'd be delighted to be his friend.'

'I have plenty of friends. I do not need any more friends, Mummy.'

'That is ridiculous, Monica. One cannot have too many friends.'

Maybe that is true when one is over thirty-five, I thought, and one's friends are beginning to die off for various reasons: but when one is my age it is very possible to have too many friends. Especially when they all fall out. It's like being a juggler – if you try to keep too many in the air at the same time, you drop some.

Of course I didn't say all that to my ageing mum, I couldn't be bothered.

'Well, Monica, if you had just arrived from another

part of the country to live here where you didn't know a living soul, *you* would like someone to offer to be your friend. Anybody would. Having no friends makes people odd, everyone knows that.'

I set down my biro with a sigh. Mother cannot understand, she says, how I can possibly concentrate on my work with the radio on, yet here she was, cheerfully rabbiting on through my English homework.

'Mind you, she smokes those funny black foreign cigarettes, they can't be healthy.'

'Who does?'

'His mother. Mrs Brolly. She sculpts. Is that the right word? Funny word.' The blind rattled as the spy behind the tin curtain pressed on a slat to see better. 'What on earth is he doing now?'

With a grand flourish I snapped shut my copy of *Under the Greenwood Tree* by Thomas Hardy and rose to see what on earth the boy from across the road was doing now. Once my mother gets a bee in her bonnet, we all get stung.

We Blakes live on a new housing development of superior semi-detached villas after the style of Swiss Chalets – I choose my words from the estate agent's glossy brochure. The houses across the road are exactly like the houses on our side of the road, they all have a pair of neat dormer windows set into steeply-sloping roofs; and each roof has, besides, a neat little square window which reflects the passing clouds. The houses were built, I'm convinced, for obsessive observers of the sky at night. All the gardens have the soft green fuzz of newly-laid lawns. Each garden is enclosed within a low wall, and the boy from across the road – no doubt in an effort to make life more interesting – had decided to walk on a wall rather than the uneven pavement. He moved along with jerks and thrusts as if an angel on high was operating him on invisible strings.

8

'That's a funny way to walk,' observed my mother.

'Hmm,' said I.

'Of course he's probably pretending to be something or other. I'm sure he's got lots of imagination, Monica.'

'Mummy, he's practising robotics.'

'Oh?'

My mother failed to understand this because she is behind the times. My science teacher, who says that women are changing, should see my mum coping with technology. A Neanderthal ape would have more gumption when it comes to setting the video.

'She's divorced. Nice-looking woman, but apparently he walked out a couple of years ago and hasn't been seen since. The boy's quite clever but he misses his dad. Sad, really, but it can easily happen if people get married too soon.'

'Message received,' I said. 'I won't get married till I'm fifty.'

'What has he got round his neck? Those are binoculars! You see? He's probably an interesting person, Monica.'

'Mummy! It is possible for one to have binoculars round one's neck, and for one to be as dull as ditchwater at the same time.'

There now followed a series of tongue-clicks and tuts. 'Oh stop being such a smarty, go and speak to the poor child. I told Mrs Brolly you would and loneliness is such a terrible thing.'

I said, 'Mother!'

'Mother' is a much more serious word than Mummy. It really means Get Off My Back and Find Something Useful To Do.

'Oh well.' The blind, now released, gave a brittle little snap. 'I can't force you to be kind to other human beings.'

'No, you can't. I am very sorry, Mummy, but you

shouldn't have set me up. It's not as if we're five year olds, you know. What would I say to him, for heaven's sake – "Welcome, New Person, fancy a game of football?"'

'Just say Hello. He'll probably let you look through his binoculars.'

Gee whizz, big fizz, I thought. 'That would be thrilling, Mother.'

'And you could talk about school. Since when were you so bird-mouthed?'

'He knows about school. Schools are all the same.'

'Oh well, that's that, then. Clear away your books and set the table for us, please.'

Daddy came home. He works as a lab assistant at the City Hospital where Mum used to be a night nurse. I think he likes the job okay, but since it involves goggling at raw samples of human beings through a microscope, the poor old dear's conversation can be rather gruesome. My father can tell you how many germs can grow in a packet of sausages overnight to the nearest ten thousand; and as for kissing, well, let's just say he can be very uncomplimentary towards the human mouth. I could tolerate his microscopic view of the world if it didn't have such dire consequences: he won't let me get a dog because, he says, the things are walking colonies of bacteria.

He had his hand up the back of my mother's jumper when I walked into the kitchen, whereupon it quickly reappeared at the end of his cuff. I sat down at table like the wise monkey who sees no evil and listened to him swear at the roads.

'They are damnable. It's a wonder I haven't wrecked the suspension of the blasted car. Six months we've been living here and still they won't tarmac the roads.'

'They're still building houses, Frank,' Mother pointed out. 'The estate isn't finished yet.'

'So what! It's not the builder's fault, if the blasted Council would get off their butts.'

'There you are, now,' Mother said mysteriously, laying down a jug of pale-green celery sticks. 'Monica, tell Raymond the tea is ready.'

I did what I was told like a good little slave girl and hollered up the stairs that the tea was ready – and Gary Kasparov appeared through his bedroom door with his pocket chess set posted about two centimetres from his nose.

'Which of you is winning?' I asked him politely, and he said, 'Beep-beep, beep-beep,' out of the side of his mouth as he passed me on the stairs.

This person was Raymond Francis Blake, my younger brother, and the noise was his Roadrunner impersonation. His repertoire includes Yogi Bear, Popeye, everybody invented by Walt Disney and his speciality is Woody Woodpecker. My brother, in recent months, has become a force to be reckoned with in our house. Why, for example, when Mother goes to the supermarket, does she always return with his favourite breakfast cereal and not mine? The answer is: she's been got at. Brother Raymond has whispered, 'Sugar Puffs please, Mum,' just as she's going through the back door. One day, when he realises that he cannot be world chess champion, he will be a rich tycoon with pots of money and no soul. Mother gets very cross when I say things like that, even though they happen to be true.

He almost started a row immediately.

'Hi, Dad – heard you come home. You must have clobbered the exhaust on a pot-hole. Hey, Mum, I hope you notice that Moan has turned me upside-down again.' ('Moan' is me, his beloved sister.)

Mother glanced at the sideboard, where my brother

11

and I sit gazing out from cardboard frames, forever frozen in our thirteenth and fifteenth years respectively. And sure enough, she saw that one of us was upside-down.

'Did you do that, Monica? Did you turn him upside-down?'

'Yes I did.'

'Well will you please stop it, it only causes silly nonsense.'

'I agree, so tell *him* to stop it,' I said with proper indignation. 'Yesterday every photograph of me in the house was turned upside-down, including the one in the hall, and you didn't say a word to him, Mummy.'

Mother looked at Father. She was passing the buck. 'You are older than he is, Monica,' Daddy uttered gravely, as if that somehow explained and excused everything. With a great show of maturity I turned the photo the right way up, and the eyes of the real IT glowed with victory.

The meal began. Daddy complimented Mummy on the quality of her mushroom soup while Kasparov played secret moves under the hem of the table-cloth. Then mother broadened the conversation.

'Well, I asked Monica to make friends with the new boy in the street today.'

'Jolly good. Nice thing to do.'

'But she didn't do it. Even though I promised the boy's mother that she would.'

'Why not?' inquired Daddy, mildly shocked.

'She has friends enough already, she claims.'

'You can't have too many friends.'

'That's exactly what I told her.'

And now Father looked at me gloomily over his tortoise-shell specs. Here was another good example of Mother acting through Father. She uses him as if he were an appliance that fits into a hoover. He couldn't care less whether I spoke more than two words to that new boy in my whole life.

'Monica, why don't you do as your mother says?'

Daddy, I thought, why haven't you got a better job with more money so that we can afford a big house with a field right round it for ponies? Naturally I couldn't verbalise all that – children cannot retaliate; it's called Cheek. We live in a world where the grown-ups have all the H-bombs.

'Daddy,' I said, 'I am not good at talking to total strangers in binoculars. Can I have a dog, please?'

'If she gets a smelly dog,' said IT, 'I want a chess computer.'

'What's wrong with binoculars I'd like to know,' said Mother.

'Damned sight better than multiple ear-rings,' mumbled Father.

I gave in. There comes a time when it just makes more sense to hunt with the hounds than run with the hare. Be a nice person, Monica, they might get you a spaniel.

'Okay! I'll go see him. I suppose Debbie and me could call over after tea and say Hello. What's his name?'

Mother began to tut-tut-tut. 'Bless me if I haven't forgotten it. Something unusual. Mrs Brolly told me but I can't remember for the life of me.'

'Well if I'm going to talk to him I have to know his name, Mummy.'

'It's Seymour,' said my brother.

'Seymour?' echoed father.

'Yeah, Seymour. He came to the chess club at lunchtime today. Just watched, though. I don't know whether he's a whizz-kid or a dodo.'

Mother didn't care whether he was a whizz-kid or a dodo, she sounded happy. 'Well I'm glad that's sorted out. Mrs Brolly will appreciate it if you call, Monica, and he's probably a nice boy – a very nice boy. Don't forget your celery, dear.'

I ate some celery. Some days it's grated carrot, other days it's nuggets of raw turnip. My parents are health freaks.

My friend Debbie is loud and coarse and common, according to my mother, and will almost certainly be obliged to be a waitress when she leaves school. Debbie does 'outrageous' things with her hair, sits with boys in the park, shrieks in public places, and 'chews' – whatever that means. My mother has actually seen Debbie on the back of a motorbike without a helmet. The bike was parked up on its stand at the time, mind you; but facts mean nothing to my mother. It's principles that count.

What is worse (according to Mother), is that I am beginning to talk just like Debbie. This feeling that I am in dire need of a higher class of friend is not shared by me. I like Debbie, she's fun and I've known her for donkey's years – since we were in primary school.

Her parents were among the first people to put down a deposit on a Swiss Chalet, so they got one of the early ones with the biggest gardens at the top of the hill. Her dad's a mechanic. The only reason they can afford a house at all (Mother says) is that Debbie's father doesn't declare the half of what he earns on his tax form. They have a Swiss Chalet courtesy of Her Majesty's Government.

At least Debbie's people aren't hygiene fanatics, I thought as I rapped on her door. They let her have a dog and they don't eat raw veg twice a week.

'Do you think I need my boots?' were her first words to me. 'Oh Gawd yes, certainly I need my boots, isn't the whole place a messy awful hole, have you read *Under the Greenwood Tree* yet, isn't it just a big yawn?

Get *back*, Collie, you daft onion. Hold him a minute, Monica, while I fetch his lead.'

I held the excited dog while Debbie got ready inside. Her preparations included a warning to her brother that she would slice off his fingers if he interfered with the video recorder. Then there followed the ceremony of clipping the lead to Collie's collar.

'Collie be good, you beast, sit still! There now, sure you're my lovely big pet . . .'

And off we set at labrador pace, Collie with his nose a centimetre from the ground, Debbie with her left arm stiff, and me trying to keep up with the pair of them. I explained how Mother had blackmailed me into an act of human kindness, and Debbie giggled.

'Come on then, maybe he's a big hunk.'

'Wrong again. I've seen him. He wears binoculars round his neck.'

'Gawd, what is there to see round here? Mud, mud and mud. Stop, Collie!' She heaved on the lead. 'Wicked dog! There's a good love!' We had come to a halt at the Brolly gate. 'What's his name?'

'Seymour.'

Debbie smiled wickedly. 'That's why he wears binoculars. See more. Get it?'

We stood there, the pair of us, laughing hysterically over that awful joke. When we had recovered I asked:

'So what are we going to say?'

'We'll say you're Monica and I'm Debbie and is Thingy in.'

'We can't call him *Thingy*.'

'Well if you ask me it's a lot better than Seymour.'

We started to laugh again, so I decided we shouldn't risk calling for Seymour Brolly for the time being – instead we continued down the hill beyond the last of the completed houses and into welly-boot country. As we negotiated bulldozer tracks brimming with watery scum, Debbie told me what Septic had been up to over the weekend. He had hoisted Farleys' bicycle up a chestnut tree and hidden it there for most of Saturday afternoon, up until the very moment when Farleys put his foot through the front door of the Police Station to report it missing. If my mother thinks Debbie is common, she should meet Septic. His latest theory is that the dinosaurs died out because of Aids. When he leaves school he intends to set up his own Kissogram company.

All of a sudden we heard a weird noise coming at us across the building site. It started up so suddenly that Debbie grabbed me by the shoulder and forced us both into a puddle. Her nails felt like teeth in my flesh. The dog, too, stiffened and began to growl in that low, scary way dogs have.

'What was that? Thunder? Oh Monica!'

I should explain that Debbie is incredibly superstitious. She believes in everything from apparitions to zombies. On Fridays the thirteenth she really behaves herself.

The noise happened again – a low, rubbery wobble like the special effects of a Spielberg film.

'It's coming from over there,' I said, pointing to a ridge of builder's rubble.

'Well I'm not going near it. That could be a spaceship.'

'For goodness sake, Debbie. Don't be so blooming corny. Come on.'

Stepping carefully through no man's land, I came to the top of the ridge and found myself overlooking a deep crater. The spaceship was, in fact, Thingy from across the road.

He was surrounded by an odd collection of objects which had been gathered – so I surmised – from all quarters of the site. Dozens of empty barrels and black plastic buckets had been lashed together with barbed wire to make a bizarre kind of fence. I couldn't tell whether Seymour Brolly had performed this peculiar feat all by himself, but he looked to me like some off-world creature preparing his nest for the night. The rumbling noise came from a sheet of metal which he wobbled in and out. His binoculars jiggled as he pranced about like a headbanger.

Then he saw Debbie and me and the dog staring down at him. I thought I might as well say something.

'Hi. My name is Monica Blake, I live almost opposite you.'

'I know. I've seen you through my binoculars.'

Well, Debbie gave me such a funny look and I knew exactly what she meant.

'You've got sparrows in your eaves already,' he said. 'Did you know that?'

'No.'

'Well you have. I'm Seymour Brolly.'

No sooner had Thingy said his name than Debbie emitted a stifled screech. This was fairly typical behaviour for Debbie – she sings 'Bor-ring' out loud when Mr Thornleigh produces the comprehension books in our English class. Seymour Brolly gazed at her for a moment or two as if she were a specimen that mildly interested him, then raised his binoculars for a closer look.

'Cut that out,' said Debbie. 'I don't want to be goggled at through those things.'

'Why not?'

'I just don't, right?'

'Okay. Would you like to see some sandmartins? They're nesting in that red sandbank over there.'

'No,' said Debbie. 'I don't like birds, they're creepy.'

Debbie has a thing about birds. If one hits your window it apparently means a death.

'Creepy? What do you mean, "creepy"? Birds have

17

the power of flight, the human race has envied them for centuries.'

'Look, I don't have to like birds just to please you, you know. If I want to fly I'll take a jumbo jet.'

I intervened. It is often my role to be a civilising influence between Debbie and the world at large.

'Debbie is a bit superstitious about birds.'

'Like Julius Caesar,' said Seymour Brolly, who picked up a plank with each hand and turned in my direction. 'Would you carry my rumble-board, please? My arms are full.'

I said I would carry his rumble-board. As we walked up the hill loaded with stuff from his den it occurred to me that I was helping him steal, and I hoped that Mother was doing her KGB act behind the iron curtain.

'Nice dog,' Seymour Brolly said to Debbie. 'Does he have a pedigree?'

'We didn't get him for nothing if that's what you mean,' came the tart reply.

We arrived, with planks and rumble-board, at the Brolly drive, where he kicked open the gate.

'Thanks a lot. Just put the tin down by the garage door. Would you like to see my garden?'

I didn't care to, actually. Gardens are for gardening, and gardening is one of those things like knitting and log tables and horse-racing that bore me witless. However, I couldn't just say, 'Sorry, Seymour, gardens are boring.'

So I said, 'Yes, why not?'

'But you'll have to go very carefully,' he said, mysteriously.

'Why?' asked Debbie. 'What's so special about your garden? Are you drilling for oil?'

'You'll see. Kindly tie your dog to the gate and follow me.'

Naturally enough, we followed him – not exactly

agog, but certainly mildly curious about what might be lurking round the corners. The first thing I spotted was the cardboard cut-out vulture on the whirligig clothesline. It was a life-size vulture, I guess (a real one I have never seen). Debbie pointed at it frantically behind Seymour Brolly's head. Her eyes were huge as he suddenly placed a forked stick in her hand.

'Keep to the path. You have been warned. Let's go.'

'What's the stick for?'

'Snakes.'

'Snakes? Suck eggs!' cried Debbie to the neighbourhood at large, and goose pimples ran up my arms. I do not like creatures without feet.

Off we set, armed with forked sticks. After several crunchy paces along a path of cinders and stones we stopped at a waterlogged hole in the ground which had a plank over it, like a bridge. Seymour Brolly spoke over his shoulder.

'Don't slip.'

'Why?'

'Alligators. And don't go near that brown patch over there, it's bottomless quicksand. Suck, slurp and you're gone.'

I heard Debbie, behind me, describe our guide as a purple onion, first class. Now we came to the large tree at the back of the garden, one of the few around here spared by the planners. Seymour Brolly gripped a trailing rope, and pointed up.

'That's where I live. My secret hut.'

'Gawd. Where's Cheetah?' said Debbie.

The hut consisted of a few planks and some branches. 'It's not very secret,' I said. 'You can see it.'

'Do you think so?'

'Of course you can see it!' Debbie raved. 'You might as well have a sign outside it saying THIS WAY TO THE

SECRET HUT. I mean, all you have to do is look UP for crying out loud.'

'People rarely do. They're too busy looking out for the alligators.' Seymour Brolly suddenly smiled at me with a huge smile that put dimples in his cheeks. He had lovely teeth. For some reason it put Debbie into an awful twist.

'Your head is definitely wired to the moon,' she said.

Seymour Brolly held up a pacifying hand. 'Okay, you win. It's not really my secret hut, it's actually a make-shift observatory. I study birds from up there.'

'I'll bet you do,' said Debbie, just as Collie began to bark at the front of the house. 'My dog wants me – you coming, Monica?'

As usual I let Debbie make up my mind for me. 'I have to go.'

'Would you like to see my axolotl? I keep it in the garage. It's real,' he added – to distinguish it from the alligators, no doubt.

'I really have to finish my English homework for tomorrow morning. An essay.'

'Fair enough. Could I have the snake-forks back, please.'

'Gawd!' breathed Debbie.

We returned his snake-forks, re-negotiated Alligator Bridge, avoided the pit of quicksand, cast a final glance at the cardboard vulture turning in the breeze, and made it back to civilisation. On the way back up the hill I wondered out loud what the devil was an axolotl?

'Something mechanical,' said Debbie, looking over her shoulder to where Seymour Brolly swayed among the branches of his tree, level with the chimney-pots. 'Monica, he is spying on us through those big peepers!' And she added one of her American words. 'The jerk!'

I was quite honest with Mother when I got home.

'Well, Monica?'

'Well, Mummy, he's a very imaginative person, just like you said.'

'I thought he might be, pet. It'll be nice for him to know young folk his own age.'

'I'm sure you're absolutely right as usual. There's a vulture sitting on his whirligig and he plays the rumble-board. Night, Mumsie, I have to finish a few pages of *Under the Greenwood Tree* for Mr T.'

For a while I struggled dutifully with our class novel. It was one of those books that suddenly seem less awful after you pass page 30 – but I would probably have found it more interesting had I not kept thinking about Seymour Brolly's back garden. Why involve Debbie and myself in his childish Amazonian fantasy? And what was he making down in that hollow? The first stage of a rocket to the moon?

I made a mental note to inform Mother over breakfast that as well as binoculars, Seymour Brolly possessed an axolotl.

Chapter

2

Our English class is an odd little gathering of assorted personalities. Some of us are high-powered intellectuals, some of us are anything but, and most of us are somewhere in between. Mr Thornleigh calls our two weekly periods 'seminars', which in my opinion is a very high-falutin' name for what actually goes on. Septic, Farleys and Debbie, to name but three, are no more interested in English Literature than they are in going bald. Jill and Martin Grey and a few others are fairly interested. Some members of the set hardly ever speak even when they're spoken to, and we also have two religious girls, Sarah and Virginia, who believe that we, the human race, won't make it into the twenty-first century. Strangely enough these two work hardest of all.

Into this batch of liquorice all-sorts stepped Seymour Brolly on Monday afternoon. His first problem, on seeing fifteen of us already seated round the table ready to Discuss, was where to park himself and his bulging grip bag. He settled for a seat beside Martin Grey and began to rummage in his pocket for writing utensils. It was so painfully obvious that he felt 'new'. The green blazer marked him out as a foreigner, so Septic regarded him as worthy of a long hard stare.

'Oi, are you the spacer who's got alligators in his back garden?'

Seymour Brolly looked up in surprise and seemed to take a firmer hold on his bag. I wondered what was in it. 'Pardon?'

'I said All-i-gate-ors.' Septic left spaces between his syllables, as if talking to someone with an ear trumpet. 'Have you got them in your back garden?'

They locked gazes for a moment or two before Seymour Brolly looked away. 'No.'

'You have so, you daft duck,' said Debbie. 'And a vulture.'

'I have an axolotl and a snake. It's a garter snake.'

'I like snakes in garters,' said Farleys, which caused Debbie to snort through her nose. She is in her element when discussing nonsense.

'Get lost, Farleys, what do you know about snakes. I hate them. They wriggle. Eeee-uk!'

'Ah, but,' said Septic wisely, 'you can't not like something just because it wriggles, can you? Because fish wriggle, and I like fish. Sarah Topping wriggles, and I love Sarah Topping.'

Sarah Topping is the pretty, religious girl with a dream figure and a face like a Hollywood nun. She hid behind a curtain of hair instead of telling Septic to curl up and die. He's trying to recruit her for his Kissogram Company.

'Read your Bible,' said Septic. 'It was your snake that changed the whole world, that's why *I* don't like snakes.'

'Explain,' said Martin Grey, drawn into the nonsense of the moment.

'Right. Who told Eve she was running around starkers in the Garden of Eden? A snake, that's who. If it wasn't for snakes the whole world would still be a nudist colony and that's a fact from the Bible. Ask Sarah, she'll tell you.'

Poor Sarah was glad to see Mr T. come through the

door before she was called upon to confirm or deny such rubbish. As copies of *Under the Greenwood Tree* hit the tabletops I reflected soberly how motherhood is not without risks. Once upon a long time ago in Septic's life he must have been a beautiful baby to whom people said Goochy goo in shops. Nowadays members of the public crossed the street to avoid him and his ghetto-blaster.

Mr Thornleigh wondered out loud how far we had progressed with our reading. He is a nice flexible man – the first to get us into a discussion group where people talk to one another and actually say what they think. Nobody is afraid of him but nobody goes wild. The oddest behaviour comes from Farleys, who after sniggering for years on end in the back row is now like a budgie out of its cage. He can't cope with the freedom. He bites his nails and laughs now and then like a hyena.

'Come on folks – somebody must have read something, you can't *all* hate Thomas Hardy. Jill?'

Jill had reached the part where the keys on somebody's clarinet froze while they were carol-singing in frosty weather. Martin Grey had read to where the choir members had just seen Fancy Day at her window.

'And you, Robert?'

Septic winced. He hates his proper name because it is a limpid thing and gives no hint of his wild, unbridled nature. 'Not too far, Sir.'

'Have you made a start? Have you read a whole page yet?'

'Sir why do I have to read this stuff?' Septic sounded as if he was in genuine pain. 'It's driving me round the bend. It's all about living in the country a million years ago and this stupid choir that sings.'

Mr Thornleigh sat down and crossed his legs. His

right shoe needed a good polish. 'Your head is nodding, Debbie. I assume this means that you agree?'

'Well, actually I think it's all very old-fashioned, Mr Thornleigh, and they talk funny.'

'Right!' Septic agreed absolutely. He opened his copy of Thomas Hardy like a scholar about to deal with the true facts. 'It doesn't even say Part One like ordinary books, it's Part the First, Part the Second, Part the Third, Part the *Fourth*.'

'Part the Fifth,' added Farleys.

'Believe me, Robert,' said Mr Thornleigh sadly, 'I weep for you. I deeply sympathise – for you and Thomas Hardy both. When he wrote *Under the Greenwood Tree* I am virtually certain that he did not have you in mind as one of his readers. On the other hand, you have made a perfectly sensible point. Here is a book that was written a hundred years ago. Can books as old as that be valuable to people today, are we asking too much of them? Can they even be interesting? Or is there some wisdom in them that keeps us turning their pages?'

Jill mentioned Charles Dickens. It turned out that Debbie had seen Nicholas Nickleby on TV and Septic had heard of Oliver Twist. Sarah Topping mentioned the Bible as something old and influential, Martin Grey threw in H. G. Wells and we ended the period discussing whether Robin Hood was real.

The bell had just gone when Mr Thornleigh turned to Seymour Brolly, who hadn't said anything other than he'd read *Gulliver's Travels*.

'I must get you a copy of *Under the Greenwood Tree* for the next seminar.'

'He can have mine, Sir,' Septic volunteered graciously.

Seymour Brolly tapped a battered old brown book at his elbow. 'It's all right, I have one of my own here.' ·

25

'Oh?' Mr Thornleigh seemed surprised. 'Did you study this text at your last school?'

'No, it was among our books at home. I enjoyed it.'

This last sentence caused a bit of a buzz. It was astonishing that he had the book at all; that he had actually read the thing seemed like a double miracle; to have enjoyed it seemed like a quantum leap.

'How would you sum it up, then?' probed Mr Thornleigh gently. 'What is the essential content of the novel? For example, it's not Science Fiction, is it?'

'It's about Fancy Day and Dick Dewey the tranter's son.' Seymour Brolly looked straight at me. For a full second I was unaccountably staring straight into his eyes before he glanced away. 'It's obviously a love story, Sir.'

'Well you could have fooled me,' Septic announced.

'I guess that wouldn't be hard,' said my new neighbour, quite deliberately.

I could swear that Mr T. smiled a huge interior smile without so much as twitching his lips. Septic sat back, looking rather puzzled in a grim sort of way, and folded his arms. As soon as Mr Thornleigh said we could go, Seymour Brolly dropped his tattered old Thomas Hardy into his grip bag, and slipped out of the room.

'Did you see him looking at you!' Debbie cried in Plantation Avenue. 'Zap. I saw him looking at you. He's got real greedy eyes.'

We were on the way home from school. 'Who, Debbie, who?'

'That spacer.'

I still didn't have a clue. 'Debbie, of whose greedy eyes are we speaking, please?'

'Lah-dee-dah! We are speaking of he what has the cardboard vulture, who else? Didn't you feel him boring into you with his eyes. Gawd, I'm surprised he needs binoculars.'

'As a matter of fact I didn't feel him boring into me with his eyes.'

'I would have. I can always tell when people are looking at me – the hairs on the back of my neck are psychic. Did you hear what he said to Septic! I mean, Monica, that was real stupid, you know what he's like.'

I did indeed know what Septic is like. He's not particularly aggressive in that he doesn't go around beating people up; on the other hand he is a large person who likes to flaunt his biceps and perform mock karate chops on lamp-posts and young trees. He is fond of using phrases like 'I'll cut you into white meat, man.' Nobody could call Septic a brainbox, but he's not stupid, either, and knows full well when he has been insulted. Seymour Brolly had failed to pick up these signals about Septic's character.

'Debbie,' I said, 'he looked at me once and our eyes met by accident. Eyes are bound to meet now and then when people sit round a table.'

'Speaking personally,' said Debbie, 'mine never met Martin Grey's once, and I spent the whole period looking straight at him. What am I going to do about him?'

Poor Debbie. Martin Grey remains blissfully unaware of the power he has to make Debbie's day. If only he would sharpen her pencil, or something, she would glow.

'Well he's very fond of sport,' I said, to be positive.

'Great! It's jolly obvious then, isn't it – I should take up rugby football.'

We were hit by an attack of the sniggers because we both hate sport. Debbie and I have the same attitude to a hockey ball – we stay well away from the thing because it's so hard and it hurts. Tennis is okay because

27

the weather is sometimes warm; but how mixed doubles with Martin Grey would dangerously swell dear Debbie's heart!

Our journey home, once resumed, was quickly interrupted once again when Debbie spotted a newspaper in one of those wire litter baskets on a lamp-post. 'Hang on a minute, I want to see my stars.'

'Debbie!'

The remains of somebody's lunch hit the gutter and a couple of crisp bags ballooned away on the breeze as the newspaper was rudely uprooted. Flick flick flick went the pages.

'Gemini. Here, listen! "Hold yourself in readiness for a major surprise that could work to your advantage. Put business before pleasure for a time even if it makes you seem a little aloof. Don't rock the boat in personal matters and you will easily weather the storms that come your way."'

The paper was lowered, and Debbie repeated in a voice that was breathless with awe, 'The storms that come your way. Oh Monica, I don't like the sound of storms that come your way.'

'Doesn't matter, Debbie love. It's yesterday's paper so they were yesterday's storms.'

'*Is* it?'

It was. We arrived home snorting.

I should have been called Polly. The first thing I do when I get home from school is put the kettle on, for I just adore tea. Neither Mum nor Gary Kasparov were in the house so I curled up beside the radiator with a cuppa and a biscuit, and read my bundle of highly sensitive correspondence.

I am absolutely certain that a deep-down part of me wants to be a spy. I have a secret. As well as ordinary old Monica Blake I am also the mysterious Miss Blunt.

People write to me about Life, and I answer their letters. Anonymously, of course.

My double-identity was Mr Thornleigh's idea. It's all to do with developing our powers of English. To give credit where it's due, he's always trying to think up fresh gimmicks to get us writing about the world as we see it. I don't think he cares very much what we write about so long as we 'use language', as he puts it.

At first I didn't want to be Miss Blunt.

'What sort of things will they write to me?' I said. 'How will I answer them? No, Mr Thornleigh I don't want to do it.'

'Of course you do, Monica, you're perfect for it – intelligent, articulate and mature.'

Soapy bubbles, I thought, doing a beamer. I like people who talk to me that way. But I still wasn't sure what it actually involved.

'It works like this, Monica. There'll be a post-box at the end of the green corridor with your name above it: MISS BLUNT. You will remain anonymous, of course. If they know who you are it won't work. I'll empty the box every so often, give you the mail, and you will write punchy replies. Be serious, though, if necessary. We'll publish the best of the letters and your replies on the notice-board.'

It began to sound like fun. 'But what will they write to me about?'

'Everything and anything, you'd be surprised. A friend of mine has tried this in another school and it works really well until the novelty wears off. Some days you can hardly get moving round the notice-board. Just for a few months, Monica, there's a good girl.'

In this way I became Miss Blunt. And now, before me, I had a fine crop of twenty-eight letters. Miss Blunt was a hit.

The first one was rather grave:

29

Dear Miss Blunt,

The Long Lane is a mess and does nothing at all for the good name of the school. They buy their crisps at the tuckie and throw the rubbish anywhere. Visitors are appalled, I'm sure. I think a bin should be provided for litter.

Yours sincerely,
Jennifer Livingstone.

The second letter was enclosed in a white envelope, from which a dead wasp fell.

Dear Miss Blunt,

I slew the first wasp of the summer yesterday and now my conscience is killing me, frankly. I keep thinking about the small deceased (which you will please find enclosed). Does this make me dangerous to human beings? I caught sight of myself in the mirror with a rolled-up newspaper in my hand and I do not believe that the look in my eyes was normal.

Fraternally yours,
Simon Joseph Baker.

I grinned to myself. I'd never known that Joe Baker was a Simon as well. The next letter was written on a fragment of jotter.

Dear Miss Blunt,

My girl friend won't let me put my hand on her knee even though it's a very nice hand. What would your advice be in this situation?

I remain,
the one-and-only,
Septic.

I drained my cup and reached for a pen, having decided already which letter should be answered first.

Dear Septic,
    Thank you for yet another wonderful letter. Try wart-remover.
        Yours, with sincerity,
            Miss Blunt.

Hardly had I written my pen name with a flourish than a battering occurred at our back door and IT made his entrance. His school-bag hit the table with a bang – one of those grey canvas things with more names scribbled over it than you would find on a leg in plaster. I pointed to a prominent Swastika, done in black marker.

'Heil Hitler.'

'That is not a Swastika,' he said shirtily. 'That is an ancient Indian good luck symbol. The Nazis got it and turned the legs the other way round, dumbo.'

He poured himself half a pint of milk and sweetened it with banana cordial. Tea is not his tipple.

'Okay Moan, you got a deal. We'll act together and put the pressure on.'

'Talk English. Are you a schoolboy or a gangster?'

'I'll support your campaign for a fleabag dog if you support mine for a chess computer. I've got a birthday coming up in a fortnight so the time is right.'

The schemer. 'No deal. You'll end up getting your computer and I'll never see my dog.'

'Possibly. But think about it. Up to now it's been three-one against a dog, this way it'll be a two-all draw. You've got a fighting chance.'

'Some chance! You wouldn't want a dog unless it played football and played chess and did your Latin homework for you.'

He fished out a glossy ad. 'There's a picture of the computer I want – make sure Mum sees it in case she walks out and buys the cheap one. You know how she likes surprises.'

Everybody likes surprises, I thought, except those of us who have a calculator instead of a heart. I glanced at the ad. Apparently the computer in question was the European Chess Computer Champion. Now whoever designed me gave me good graphics – I have a pop-up mind – and a mental picture hit me of all these machines playing chess against one another and I wondered what the world was coming to.

'Got it all figured out, haven't you?'

'Look, you don't want any old dog, I don't want a computer without a pedigree. I was talking about you at lunch-time today.'

'Who with?'

'Seymour Brolly.'

'What did he say?'

'Wanted to know if you played chess. I told him you hadn't a baldy clue.'

'Many thanks. What did you think of him?'

'Boy, he's some player. He nearly did Mr Wilson with a Ruy Lopez.'

Gee whizz, big fizz. I wanted details of a different sort. 'Raymond, I am talking about personality, I am talking about character and charm, I am referring to his qualities as a human being – not whether he can do people with a Ruy Lopez.'

A crafty smile appeared on my brother's face. 'Why, do you fancy him? For a small fee I could let him know you're available.'

I took up my pen, and wrote the word MORON between the spokes of his swastika.

Chapter

3

I love getting letters – real letters I mean, not the Agony Aunt variety. I love the fluttery feeling that comes over me when I wonder, just for a minute, who in the big wide world could possibly be writing to insignificant little me. When I was small I longed to find a note in a bottle or have a pigeon fly in with a message on its leg only for me.

When I came down the stairs on Thursday morning mother said, 'Monica, there's something on the table for you behind the phone, did you see it?'

'No, what kind of something?'

'It feels like an invitation. Maybe one of your friends is having a party, dear.'

Naturally I was pleased for a moment. Then I noticed that the envelope had no stamp, which meant that it hadn't travelled far. I like my letters to come from faraway places with strange-sounding names.

There was no address; only MONICA BLAKE on the outside.

'Well? Aren't you going to open it?' Mother had followed me into the hall, and now hovered. I tied the trailing belt ends of her flannel dressing-gown round her waist. 'You look a sight. Hasn't it occurred to you, Mummy, that this communication to me might be personal?'

'Don't be so silly, Monica,' was the reply, which seemed to suggest that I was in no way a person yet. I opened the letter with a long-suffering sigh and we read it together.

You are cordially invited to become a friend of the blue whale.
Seymour Brolly.

Mother regarded me with studiously angled eyebrows. Here was food for thought, and she was having a meal. Then she read the words again.

'What does it mean?'

'I do not have a lulu,' I replied truthfully.

'Monica, you must know, surely. How can you not? It says whales.'

'Not exactly. It says whale. Only one. A blue one.'

'Well what does whale mean?'

'Mummy, I do not know what this note means, I know nothing about whales. Until this moment I did not know that one of them is blue and I cannot imagine how anyone can possibly be its friend. And now I have to eat my breakfast because you don't allow me to go to school on an empty stomach.'

'I should think not – that's the way to faint.'

I swilled down some of IT's favourite cereal, and left for school.

Going to school is the dreariest thing I do – those grey, leaden mornings really feed me some beautiful, positive thoughts: such as what's it like to be old? Do people really think of death after they've made love? Should I know how to kill myself in case I get cancer? Going to school makes me feel like some meek little creature who has been wound-up and set in motion at the appointed time. Mr Crothers down the road always seems to open his garage door as I am passing, and the same queue of cars waits for gaps in the traffic, and the same three women in uniforms wait outside the bank for the manager to arrive with his keys. It's all so blooming inexorable, I thought, one day after another, tick after tock until they put the pennies on your eyes. Life is just a way of passing the time.

I saw Septic stop his bike obediently at the lights and heard Miss Irons ringing the hurry-bell in the distance. Traffic-lights, hurry-bells and people, all cogs together in a great big wound-up watch.

Watch it Monica, I thought, you didn't used to have such thoughts, you were immune. Growing up is a disease we all catch, Peter Pan is dead.

Debbie, who gets a lift, was waiting for me at the gate with a white envelope in her hand. 'Look what I got! First thing this morning. It was just lying on the carpet! He must have sneaked up our path this morning and stuck in through the letter-box and what's he playing at, I'd like to know?'

I held up my note. 'Snap!'

'Oh thank the stars, I thought it was only me. Whales! What is this all about?'

'I don't know, Debbie, do I? Let's find him and ask him.'

There was no sign of Seymour Brolly, however. He wasn't in our Maths class that morning, so we reckoned that they must have stuck him in with the Silicon Chip lot – the high fliers. Eventually he turned up in our English class just before lunch.

Mr Thornleigh organised us into groups and presented us with a passage in which every sixth word had been blanked out. Our task was to find suitable words instead of the blanks – the perfect opportunity for Debbie to tackle Seymour Brolly with an aggressive whisper.

'Hey, did you send us a note about whales?'

'Yes, blue whales.'

'Never mind the colour, Spacer, I don't care if they're pink and yellow – why?'

'They're an endangered species, I thought you might be interested.'

'In what.'

'Saving them,' said Seymour Brolly.

He was rewarded with one of Debbie's inimitable stares. 'Well for your information we are not interested, are we, Monica? We've never seen a whale and we don't give a fig about whales, you drunk duck. And another thing, don't stick notes through my door, I don't like it. Here.'

She returned his note after neatly dividing it into quarters. Seymour Brolly blushed, but there was no relief. 'At least your blood's red, Spacer, I was beginning to wonder if you came from the Milky Way.'

'I do.'

'What?'

'And so do you, it's our home galaxy.'

Just as Debbie – so I suspected – was getting out of her depth, a long shadow appeared over our table.

'Is this a family row,' said Mr Thornleigh, 'or can any old body join in?' He retrieved the note, pieced it together and read the contents impassively.

'Hmm. The blue whale.'

'Mr Thornleigh, I want you to know that that doesn't belong to me. *He* stuck it through my door this morning and he sent Monica one too, didn't he, Monica?'

Thanks Debbie, you're a real friend for roping me in. I glared at Septic, who was leering at all of us. That zombie needs trouble and fuss to bring him alive the way a vampire needs blood.

Suddenly Seymour Brolly's hand darted to the inside pocket of his new blazer. 'I have a letter here from my

Member of Parliament, Sir. You will see that it's written on House of Commons notepaper.'

Apparently this was so – Mr T.'s nodding head confirmed it.

'I'm very concerned, you see,' continued Seymour Brolly, 'about the declining population of whales, so I have started a society to protect them. Naturally I wrote to my M.P. about whale-hunting.'

'Naturally,' repeated Mr Thornleigh.

'I knew a whale once,' said Septic. 'His name was Moby Dick.'

'Shut up, Glover,' said Mr Thornleigh, who sometimes speaks to Septic in very basic English. 'Go on, Brolly.'

'And my M.P. wrote back, Sir. You'll see in his letter that he blames the Japanese in particular, who refuse to accept quotas. They just keep on killing whales.'

Mr Thornleigh said, 'I see,' and turned to the other party in the controversy. 'And you do not wish to become a friend of the blue whale, Debbie?'

'Suck eggs!' cried Debbie, and Mr Thornleigh winced.

'Suck eggs. Interesting. Your command of the language, Debbie, becomes more marvellous with each passing day.' He turned to me. 'What about you, Monica?'

I didn't answer and I don't know why, I had the weirdest feeling that Seymour Brolly was sitting on the edge of his seat, sending out mind-waves, pleading for empathy. Was I psychic like the hairs on the back of Debbie's neck or simply identifying with the underdog?

Then I spoke. 'I don't honestly see what I can do about the Japanese, Mr Thornleigh. But it would surely be a pity if there were no whales.'

Debbie looked at me darkly, for she expects total loyalty from her friends and compromise is not a concept she understands. Mr Thornleigh gave one of his mysterious little Mona Lisa smiles and put us back to filling in the blanks.

I can reveal that by the end of school that day I was sick of whales. I didn't know whether to blame Seymour Brolly and his Member of Parliament, or those twin goons Septic and Farleys, who produced a torrent of jokes about whales and Wales. One of these – 'What kind of a football team have whales?' – put Farleys into such a kink that he got himself slung out of French.

When I got home I thought I had finished with whales. At tea Mummy and Daddy discussed whether the grass on our front lawn was growing faster than the grass on next door's lawn. Apparently ours had its nose in front by a millimetre or two, but it was a yellower shade of green. And weedier. Mother complained bitterly about a footprint she had discovered in a flower-bed, and spoke grimly about 'those scruffy new milkmen'. I sat there wondering whether my married life would ever be as exhilarating as this; then I went upstairs to do some Geography.

Students of Geography will know what I mean when I say that Geography never ends, there is too much of it, it simply goes on for ever and ever. The more you do, the more it threatens to bury you deep down under layers of sedimentary, igneous or metamorphic rocks. I was almost relieved when mother came into the room and told me that there was a person at the door for me.

'Who? Debbie?'

'No, it's that boy. He says he would like a word with you. And he's still wearing those things round his neck. Do you think he ever takes them off?'

My mother sounded bemused, as if she were beginning to have her doubts about Seymour Brolly. Perhaps the axolotl was the last straw. Serve her right.

'I'll see what he wants. It's probably something about school.'

In the glass porch at the front of our Swiss Chalet there is a large clay pot filled with geraniums. By the time I got downstairs Seymour Brolly had come into the porch and was now bent double over the pot in a pose of deliberation.

'They look a bit straggly,' he said. 'You could take nice cuttings off those.'

'They're Mum's. I hate them, they smell like cat's pee.'

'Everybody says that about geraniums,' he said – and just stood there.

Should I invite him in, I wondered? I am hopeless at protocol. I decided that Yes, I should. As he stepped into the hall he tapped the photograph of me on the wall.

'Why is this hanging upside-down?'

I set my photo to rights, inwardly cursing my oaf of a brother. So war had broken out again. Right!

'Raymond thinks I look better that way.'

'It's a very nice photograph. Very natural.'

'Thank you. They say the camera never lies.'

'No, indeed.'

There was a silence now, during which Mother hauled the hoover through the hall and grinned stupidly at each of us in turn before passing into the kitchen.

'I've actually called with these,' he said, producing two slim white tickets like a magician. 'They're Mummy's tickets really, but she has a tutoring class that night and . . .'

And nothing more. His speech tailed off and all I could hear was the theme from Eastenders.

'What are they for, your . . . tickets?'

'Oh, just a concert. We got them for nothing, so please say No if you want to. It's just an idea.'

'Who is it?'

39

'A BBC studio orchestra. They're playing pieces by Mozart, Rossini and Shostakovitch.'

My brain went into graphic mode. Up popped Debbie, aghast, crying aloud. 'Gawd! Music for the over forties!' I was breathless.

'I think, maybe . . . I've never been to a concert before.' (Certainly not starring those three gents, I might have added.) 'It might be a bit, well, *heavy* for me.'

'What do you mean by "heavy"?'

'I suppose I mean it's serious. Serious music.'

'No it's not. Not all of it.'

By this time I was feeling penned in. I couldn't think straight, my back had made physical contact with the wall.

'It's classical, then. It's classical music.'

'So what,' he said. 'You can't stay a teeny-bopper all your life.'

Seymour Brolly smiled. It may have been a supercilious smile or it may not have been – I didn't give him the benefit of the doubt. 'What's that supposed to mean? That I've got bad taste in music, or something?'

'Not at all. It just means that we all grow up, musically speaking. People don't stay heavy-metal headbangers all their lives.'

'You sound,' I said, 'like my grandad.'

His head dropped. 'This wasn't a good idea,' he said suddenly. 'I see that now. I'm sorry.'

He popped the tickets into his mouth and set his jaws in motion as if he had jelly-babies in there. Still chewing, he left.

He'd just asked me out! Hadn't he? Mother came out and found me in the hall like a rooted geranium. 'Did you get things sorted out all right, love?'

No Mother, I didn't, I shrieked inside my head. The whole business was oddly upsetting.

'Yes, Mum' I said. 'He came over to invite me to a concert.'

'Really?'

'No drink, drugs or groupies, Mother – music by Shostakovitch. I said No. And anyway, he ate the tickets.'

Geography wasn't quite the same after that, I couldn't concentrate properly. Question: when was the last time someone invited you out, Monica? Answer: six months ago a boy from the Youth Club took me to the pictures. He was quite a nice-looking sort, what Debbie calls a bit of a poser. He wore his shirt-tail out rather than in and he'd just bought himself a fifty-pound snooker cue. Anyway, when we came out of the movie he produced comments such as 'sunnuvabitch' and 'make my day' like a Clint Eastwood clone and I just wanted to go home. I gave him the brush-off.

Now here I was, turning my back on Seymour Brolly and Shostakovitch. You're a real Seeker After Experience, Monica, said a sarcastic little gremlin inside my head.

Wouldn't it be nice, though, I thought, to be like Debbie and have a Martin Grey to be dying about?

PART

2

Chapter

1

On Saturday morning I was full of the joys of Spring until I saw what had been sellotaped to the headboard of my bed, which now resembled a tombstone.

HERE LIES THE BODY
OF MONICA BLAKE.
IN LIFE SHE WAS FAT,
NOW SHE'S A RAKE.

Ignore him, Monica, I counselled, count up to ten, do not embark on ambitious schemes of violent revenge, he *is* your little brother. Besides, you are not fat, you are generously proportioned – a proper armful, one might say.

During the descent to breakfast I not only turned his picture upside-down, I also faced it to the wall. It was petty, of course, but the best I could think of in the short term.

He greeted me with, 'Morning, Moan.'

'Stay out of my sunshine, bonehead, or I'll pickle your brain.'

'Monica!' Mother ejaculated, entering in a pair of dramatic red gardening gloves. 'That is terrible talk to your brother. Go and help Daddy in the front garden if you've nothing better to do.'

'He can't be weeding the lawn already.'

'He is not weeding the lawn, he is planting a hedge.'

Naturally I wolfed down my breakfast to get out there and pitch in. Daddy was bent double beside a barrow full of compost and he seemed to be planting dead sticks. I asked, 'Can I help, Daddy?' and he straightened up like something that needed oiling.

'No thanks, Pet. I can manage.'

It was a labour of love, obviously, that hedge. I wasn't at all offended, this was something Daddy wanted to do all by himself alone – in five years' time people would know when they were leaving the outside world and entering Blake country. Males are territorial creatures, I mused; little birdies sing, daddies plant hedges.

While I was enjoying these idle speculations Seymour Brolly appeared at our fence and said, 'Hi there.'

Daddy said Good Morning and I said Hello. We both looked hard at the cardboard tube in his hand. It resembled the inside of a very, very wide roll of loo paper.

'Can I speak to you for a minute or two, Monica?'

'Well, yes,' I said. 'I guess so.'

In this way we went walking together in the watery sunshine of a spring day. I was careful to steer us down the hill rather than up in case we collided with Debbie, who would certainly have more than enough to say if she spotted us.

'I see you're putting down a box hedge,' he said. 'The box is very slow-growing, but it's an excellent subject for topiary.' Something to do with bees, I thought? 'We used to have a box hedge at our last house, you should have seen it in the autumn. There were millions of spiders' webs all over it, like a finely-made shawl, glistening with dew.'

'Very nice,' I said.

46

'It was, rather.'

This was the kind of conversation, I felt sure, which must have been popular in the green and pleasant country lanes of a hundred years ago and more, in the days of *Under the Greenwood Tree*. It was a pity about the JCB behind us, bigger than an elephant. Thomas Hardy couldn't have clapped his eyes on many of those.

Seymour Brolly produced his cardboard tube. 'I thought you might like to see this petition. I have it in this cardboard tube in case it gets dog-eared.'

'A petition? You mean for names?'

He nodded. 'I'll be sending it eventually to the Emperor of Japan.'

I didn't know how to react to that information other than stand there vacantly like an actress awaiting a prompt from the wings. The words Emperor of Japan rattled in my brain like three dried peas in an old tin can.

'What is your petition about?' I inquired after a pause.

'I'll show you.'

The contents of the tube were removed forthwith and unfurled before my eyes. The scroll was most beautifully presented in black italic writing and contained enough space for five hundred signatures.

'It calls on the Japanese to conform to international practice and conventions with regard to the killing of whales.'

'Really?'

Glory-be, I was thinking madly, he'll ask me to sign it and what'll I say? He had two signatures on that thing, only two in all those empty spaces and I had no wish to appear on his petition at all, let alone in third place.

'Yes. It's not much, of course, but a large number of small gestures can help. As you pointed out in class the other day, it's a matter of bringing pressure on the guilty parties.'

47

I hadn't said any such thing!

'Would you like to sign it, Monica? Public opinion can be very powerful.'

Quite frankly I began to gush. I did not want my opinion made public, whatever it was. 'Well I don't know, I'm not really sure. I mean I don't have an opinion as such, not a serious one anyway. It's not like fox-hunting when you think about it, is it, because, well . . . I've seen foxes. I think. And it might not be fair to your petition if I didn't know all the . . . eh, the facts. Has anyone else signed it? Debbie?'

'I haven't asked her. I would though, if I thought she might sign.'

And pigs might fly, I thought.

'Look – I'll think about it, that's all I can say. Okay?'

'Sure. Perhaps in a few days.' He looked down at me with keen eyes and smiled lightly – he really did have a nice smile. Out of school uniform he seemed somehow taller, and older. 'Thanks for your time, Monica. Bye.'

And he sounded so quietly civilised. Perhaps Mother is right, I thought with dismay – 'Good manners are so *very* important in a person, Monica.'

Having walked me to the bottom of the hill, Seymour Brolly kept right on going and abandoned me there. There was nothing for it but to trudge back up the hill again. Mother glanced up from her weeding, blatantly curious. 'Was that Seymour Brolly you were with, dear?'

I could see that he was beginning to fascinate her in some peculiar way. 'Yes, Mummy – minus binoculars. He's getting up a petition to send to the Emperor of Japan and he wants me to sign it.'

'My stars! What about?'

'Whales.'

'And did you?'

'No.'

My Mum's face, at that moment, deserved to be painted.

Debbie and I spent quite a time during the next few days avoiding Seymour Brolly and his petition to Japan.

On Wednesday, for a laugh, we kept him under surveillance at break-time, and it was actually quite interesting to see him standing with one foot on either side of his grip bag, feeding his face with crisps while his other hand held the glasses to his eyes. Turning slowly like one of those big metal dishes that listen to the universe, and completely oblivious to his fan club of first-formers, he scanned the streets and roof-tops of the great beyond, searching for . . . we didn't know what.

'Blooming blue whales,' suggested Debbie.

I found it hard to believe that over there stood a person who had a letter from the British House of Commons in his pocket and a petition to Japan in his bag.

'Debbie.'

'What, my duck?'

'How will he send it, that petition? You can't look an Emperor up in the yellow pages, can you?'

'On a slow boat to China for all I care. Watch it, he's turning our way.'

We ducked behind a pillar and sniggered unharmoniously for a while. 'You have to admit,' I said, 'he's not your average run-of-the-mill citizen, is he?'

'Monica, neither was Frankenstein, but you still wouldn't fancy a bolt through your neck, would you? And where does the spacer come to live? Right up our street! Gawd!'

Lunch-time on Wednesday is Miss Irons' choir-practice day. Debbie is in the choir, and so am I. The truth is that I don't particularly want to be in the choir, though it's quite nice to dress up in white blouses and royal-blue skirts for big performance nights. Debbie doesn't want to be in the choir, either – Martin Grey doesn't sing – but we were both chosen personally by Miss Irons.

Mere pupils do not decide whether they are to be in the choir or out of it – no way. What happens is that Miss Irons gives you a test, and if you don't want to be in the choir you should flunk the test by croaking like a frog: but you don't. When Miss Irons is looking down your tonsils you try to sing like a nightingale – or, rather, a linnet. People, Miss Irons sometimes says, are either frogs or linnets.

She terrifies people. Even the Head creeps into her room as if he's back in short trousers. People don't dare whisper when passing by her window because she's like one of those spiders that can feel vibrations, and is very likely to rush out and bite your head off.

Anyhow, on this particular Wednesday the chosen few waited patiently for her to finish her after-dinner coffee when the door opened and the usual hush came over the company.

It was only Seymour Brolly in his binoculars. He said Hello to us and I said Hello back and Debbie's lips smiled the shortest smile in human history. Nevertheless he sat down beside her.

'Is this where the choir meets?'

Debbie stretched out a toe towards the piano. 'Point your goggles at that.'

'Thank you. I like singing. I used to sing at my last school.'

'Have you seen Miss Irons about joining?' I asked pleasantly, to make conversation.

'No.'

Debbie and I stared at one another, great minds thinking alike.

'Hey wait there a minute, Spacer, drop anchor – have you been tested?'

'What for?'

'Singing!' said Debbie. 'There are linnets who can sing like us and frogs who only croak. Which are you?'

The door opened before he could answer and Miss Irons appeared. Carefully cuddling a mug in the palms of her hands, she sat down at the piano. Now, with her fingers thawed, she waggled them over the keys like a witch casting a spell, and began to play.

'That is the introduction, remember? Let us try the first verse through once. And begin. One and two and . . .'

It was a song about the Rio Grande. After one line it stopped, and Miss Irons squirmed sideways on her stool.

'There is a foreign body in our midst,' she said.

With lips pursed like the school nit nurse examining a suspect head, she scanned the rows of seats until her eyes locked on to Seymour Brolly.

'Take those things off at once!' was her opening salvo. She meant the binoculars, of course. 'Who do you think you are – the captain of a ship?'

'No, Miss Irons, actually I . . .'

'What are you doing here?'

'I made some inquiries, you see, and I was told that the choir meets here.'

'This is where the choir meets. I asked what are *you* doing here?'

'I like to sing, Miss Irons. I was in the choir at my last school.'

'Were you.' The eyes continued to stare, but Seymour Brolly refused to shrivel up and die. 'In *this* institution music is not a frivolous pursuit, it is dedicated to the pursuit of nothing short of excellence. Sing these notes.'

She played four of them – doh-me-soh-fah, I think.

Seymour Brolly sang them out with great confidence and it seemed to me that he got pretty close. But I do not have absolute pitch like Miss Irons.

'In this school,' she said, 'we like to think that we reward merit in all its forms. Whatever form your merit takes, it is clearly not musical. You are one of life's frogs, boy – go and play football.'

This was a good example of Miss Irons letting a pupil down gently. Seymour Brolly failed to get the message.

'But I want to be in the choir.'

'You cannot be in the choir, you have to be able to sing.'

'But you are a teacher, Miss Irons,' came the incredible reply. 'Surely it is your job to teach me. You will find me a very willing pupil.'

I caught sight of Debbie's face, and I guess it must have been a mirror-image of my own. This was gripping stuff, real-life soap, and we were right there in the front seats. Miss Irons quietly closed the lid of her piano, and up she rose.

'What did you just say to me?'

'I said that I am very willing to learn.'

'How dare you come into this room and talk to me like that. The cheek of it, telling me what my job is! Who do you think I am, boy, a *fish*wife?' Her voice zoomed up an octave on the word fish, partly because she had Seymour Brolly's collar by then, and had hauled him to his feet. He was taller than she, but still she frog-marched him to the door and personally expelled him into the corridor beyond with the manner and expression of one emptying out the grotty contents of a hoover bag. Then she turned, dusted her palms together and settled once more on the piano stool.

'Let us continue. All together, please, one and two and . . .'

We were bound for the Rio Grande.

Chapter

2

'I'm telling you the facts,' said Farleys. 'The facts, the facts. He's got forty names to send away to Japan, they're all there on his big sheet with the fancy writing. My sister's seen it. Maybe he's even got fifty.'

It was break-time, and bucketing outside, so we were spending break in the English seminar room. Some of us were nervous because Septic twiddled a sprig of plastic mistletoe in his right hand.

'They're probably all faked,' said Debbie. 'I'll bet he wrote all those names himself, the telephone book's full of them. And if you come near me with that mistletoe, Septic, you'll need crowns on your front teeth.'

Septic grinned with delight. 'This is an old custom. If you've got mistletoe you've got pagan rights.'

'Eat your spinach, Popeye!'

'I am waiting for somebody with class,' declared Septic.

Poor Sarah Topping, I thought.

'I'm telling you, they're real,' continued Farleys. 'He lets the first-formers peep through his glasses if they'll sign on the dotted line. They're queueing up.'

'The cheater!' cried Debbie. 'He's bribing people to be friends of whales!'

'The Emperor of Japan isn't going to know that,' I said.

'That's why he's a cheat. The Emperor of Japan gets a whole lot of names in the post one fine day and he thinks to himself, Oh, all those people over there are mad keen on whales – when all they wanted was to look through Spacer's glasses. Don't you think that's *evil*?'

I stifled an attack of minor convulsions. There is something totally unconvincing about my Deborah when she gets uptight about grave moral issues.

'Who is he anyway,' wondered Septic, 'the Emperor of Japan?'

'A foreigner, Septic, you wouldn't know him,' explained Debbie.

Sarah Topping appeared with her friend and stared in horror not only at Septic, but also at the sprig of mistletoe now hovering over his head. It performed an inviting little twirl, like the blades of a mini-helicopter.

'Sarah,' he begged, 'would you please kiss me with your lips like velvet?'

'Tell the nutcase to Get Lost, Sarah,' advised Debbie. 'It's the month of May, not blooming Christmas.'

'Every day is like Christmas for Sarah and me. Tell them, Sarah.'

She didn't have to tell us, fortunately, because Seymour Brolly came into the room at that moment and created a diversion. Septic winked at Farleys, who grinned back as if they had something arranged between them. David Attenborough should make a programme about those two: being lower primates, no words are necessary, non-verbal communication is enough.

'Hey, Spacer,' said Septic. 'Let's have a look at your petition to Japan.'

A pause occurred, which I didn't like much. Seymour Brolly seemed to feel that he required a careful reply.

'My name is not Spacer.'

'Okay, okay, keep your shirt on. What do you think of elephants?'

'Why?'

'Farleys and me – we like elephants. Do you like elephants?'

No answer came, the question was loaded with something. Overtones. Seymour Brolly blinked a few times and looked at me, briefly. Farleys, meanwhile had crept towards the grip bag with some purpose in mind. The petition, I guessed.

'Here's what I think,' said Septic. 'If you stop people shooting whales they're just going to start shooting elephants, aren't they? All those people with nothing left to shoot are just going to head straight for Africa. What's the sense in that? I'd rather have no whales than no elephants, you're not being fair, Spacer. Who should I write to if I want to save the elephants?'

'Tarzan,' suggested Debbie.

'I got them!'

With a crow of delight Farleys plucked the binoculars from the bag and tossed them half-way across the room to Septic.

'Nice case they're in, Spacer. Very jazzy indeed, I have to say.' He made for the window and a view. 'Hey, these are some peepers. Whee, there's truck driver half a kilometre away and he's picking his nose. Anybody want a look?'

Debbie accepted the glasses eagerly, and after a quick look passed them on to me. I could feel my face doing a roast without having the faintest clue why. It was ridiculous, I felt like a traitor to be handling the things – yet how could I and why should I, I hardly knew him. But neither could I bear to be a spoilsport and end up on the sharp end of Debbie's tongue.

Curiously, Seymour Brolly didn't seem to mind as much as I did, he sat there quietly doodling on a piece of paper. The binoculars had returned to Septic when Mr T. walked in.

'Ah. You've taken up a new hobby, Robert.'

'Whaddyamean?' replied the lower primate.

'I mean the field glasses. A fairy godmother has waved her magic wand and hey presto! – you've turned into an ornithologist. Truly, miracles never cease.'

Septic frowned, a sure sign of mental pain. 'Ornithologist' was giving him bother. 'Spacer lent me these glasses, didn't you, Spacer?'

Seymour Brolly fixed him with a long, cold stare, and his voice matched it. 'No. I didn't lend them to you. You took them out of my bag. And they cost over two hundred pounds. And if you break them or scratch the lenses I'll sue you in the courts until I get every penny of my money back.'

I'm only guessing, of course, but that appeared to have been the first time that anybody had ever threatened to take Septic to court. It was rather different from someone threatening to bring up a big brother to work him over – Septic was facing a judge in a funny gown and a fancy wig.

But you have to admire Septic, sometimes. He set the glasses on Seymour Brolly's table as if he was doing a friend a favour. 'What are we doing in English, Mr Thornleigh,' he asked with a healthy appetite for work. 'Can we have drama please, Sir?'

There was drama all right, but as far as I'm concerned it happened in our house after tea and not in school. Mother came down the stairs all of a flutter and walked into the living-room like Big Chief Grim-in-the-Face. She held a page of mine between finger and thumb as if it was unclean.

In a sense, I suppose it was. I accepted the trembling sheaf into my hands and immediately closed my weary

56

eyes. She had come across my latest batch of letters to Miss Blunt – and of course, whose happened to be on top of the pile . . . ?

Dear Miss Blunt,
    About my girlfriend's knee and my warts. I don't have warts for your information, my hands are in perfect condition for caressing legs and thighs. Thighs are smooth. Thighs are beautiful. I don't think you understand what it's like to be sexy like me and you're probably a frigid old goat.
    I am,
      Septic.

You careless twit, Monica, I thought. Shut Your Bedroom Door At All Times – it's an elementary rule of growing up. Quite apart from the contents of the letter, it was decorated in the margins and corners with many doodles, and not all of these were decent.

In some houses this sort of thing would have been no big cheese, but I knew Mother – this was not the sort of thinking that made our country great. Even Daddy stopped paging the Oracle and gave the coming event some attention.

'It's nothing, Mummy. It's just part of our Use of English course, that's all.'

'English? Monica, nobody in their right mind could possibly call this English. I went to school, too, you know. What happened to the kind of English I used to do, has it died out altogether?'

I got quite technical, explaining how the whole exercise was nothing more than a Vehicle for Self-expression, an Outlet for the Inner Monologue bubbling up inside all of us – it was not to be taken seriously, it was fun.

57

'Some fun! "Thighs are beautiful".' (Father gave a start in his chair.) 'What kind of fun is that? In my day English was speech marks and nice poetry and grammar and things.'

'It is, it still is. The thinking is nowadays that students can't just write in a vacuum, they need an audience, someone to write *for*, someone who's going to read their work. It's all about motivation, Mummy. They write to me and I write back. I'm Miss Blunt.'

'Why does it have to be you?'

'Mr Thornleigh picked me specially because I'm so mature.'

'How can you be?' Mother flopped into a chair. 'Only a couple of years ago you wouldn't let me get your hair cut, you said you wanted to be a little girl for ever, you wanted to be able to sit on it. That seems like yesterday, and now you're answering those . . . those problems.' She turned to my bewildered father. 'She's answering everybody's problems.'

The letter landed on his lap.

I left with all the dignity I could muster to fetch the rest of my Miss Blunt letters. This scene was a perfect example of how Mother gets carried away by the tides of life. Somewhere in some bland magazine she had read, no doubt, how difficult modern teenagers can be and how impossible it is to be the mother of one. Hence her reference to the length of my hair light years ago. Father is less complicated. If you can keep on passing exams you can't go wrong, even if you are a modern teenager.

'Daddy,' I said on my return, 'that is the only letter you could possibly object to and it was written by a complete and utter fool. Septic is Robert Glover and he hasn't got a girlfriend – he hasn't even got warts. Most of them are sensible, people air their views about all kinds of things. Here's one, look.'

Dear Miss Blunt,

    I have noted that many of your replies to your correspondents are facetious in tone, but I shall risk that. Your readers may not be aware that an entire species of ocean-going mammals may be hunted to extinction unless action is taken. I refer to the Blue Whale. Since public opinion is sometimes important in such matters, pupils may make known their views by signing a petition I have prepared for sending to the Japanese authorities.

    Yours sincerely,

    Seymour Brolly.

'You see, Daddy? Whales are a genuine problem. They're a world-wide problem. I get letters about politics and sport and the environment and everything, you've no idea how terribly educational it all is.'

'Hmm,' mumbled Father. 'This teacher must think you're good at English. That's why he chose you.'

'Absolutely. You are absolutely correct, Daddy.'

'Then I suppose it's all right.' He glanced cagily at Mother, who was engrossed in Seymour Brolly's letter. 'There doesn't seem to be too much of a problem, dear.'

Mother's face resolved itself into a mask of serene indifference, illustrating to perfection the kind of sophisticated huff she can pull when the voting goes against her. 'Well if you ask me, it's a funny way to teach anybody anything.'

Among other things, we were discussing Thomas Hardy's use of imagery in *Under the Greenwood Tree*. The bell to end morning lessons had long since gone, but while the rest of us lusted after food and freedom, Mr Thornleigh, it seemed, was stuck in the nineteenth century.

59

'Listen,' he said, 'here's another one: "A curl of woodsmoke drooped over the roof like the blue feather in a lady's hat." Do you like that one? Can you see it? Roof and hat. Blue smoke and feather. Well?'

'Ah come on, Sir,' said Septic. 'We're gonna get no dinner.'

A quick glance at his wrist told Mr Thornleigh that this was so. He apologised, which I thought was nice of him, and we made a bee-line for the canteen.

I do not normally sit down to eat with Septic and Farleys, but on this particular day I could not help it. The teacher on duty steered us all, by means of a scowl, towards the same table because we were so late.

We had to choose salad, which put Septic in bad form. The lower primates like to feed on raw meat. 'If I was Desperate Dan they'd feed me cow pie. What use is this stuff to a body like mine?'

For dessert we had a cube of shortbread set on a wobbly sea of pale-green jelly. Septic, like a predator cropping for all corn, noticed that Seymour Brolly made no effort to eat his.

'What's wrong with your jelly, Spacer?'

'I don't eat jelly.'

Septic's spoon twitched. 'So what are you going to do with it?'

'Leave it.'

'Really? Sling it over here and I'll shift it for you.'

'No.'

Most of us were amazed. It was an Over-My-Dead-Body sort of reply.

'Let him eat the jelly, you selfish beast,' Debbie said delicately.

'I told you, I do not eat jelly – it's derived from whales.'

'Is it?' Septic glanced down at his empty plate. He looked happy. 'Stone me, we've been eating Moby

Dick! Did you know that, Farleys? Ah come on, Spacer, gimme your jelly like a good lad, they're only going to dump it in the bin.'

With these words he reached forward and took hold of the plate – at which point Seymour Brolly spat an ugly spreading spittle over the food.

I never heard a dinner table go so quiet. You could easily hear bits of conversation from three or four tables away. Even Debbie was speechless after a short little squeal. Septic lurched backwards like somebody struck, and sat there very still and pale as if the spit had landed on his person.

'Wait till you get out of here, boy,' he said through taut lips. 'I'm going to screw up your face, you ignorant pig.'

It was my job, as server at the head of the table, to scrape the remains into a dish. As I flicked the jelly off Seymour Brolly's plate I wondered what could be going on inside his head. Surely he must realise he'd stepped over the line.

But there was no way out for him. Septic wasn't an out-and-out thug by any means – in fact, I do believe that he'd begun to have a grudging sort of respect for Seymour Brolly – but he certainly wasn't beyond biffing people if he thought a biff was needed. Farley leaned back on two legs of his chair and passed the good news to the table behind him. Big fight.

The canteen emptied. Ours was the last table out bar one. Seymour Brolly shuffled out first with his grip bag under his arm like a set of bagpipes, then came Farley, Septic and Debbie, who tugged breathlessly at my arm. 'Get your skates on, honeybun, or we'll miss it.'

Seymour Brolly hurried down the outer wall of the canteen and turned left along the gable as if trying for a quick getaway. Wise move, I thought. Then he stopped, and within seconds found himself trapped behind a barrier of jostling bodies. The jungle drums must have been working overtime, for there were dozens of people present already. Some cheeky little first-formers crawled through our legs and popped-up like grinning rabbits in front of me and Debbie, who said, 'Beat it or you're dead.' After that we had a good view, although I wasn't too sure that I wanted to watch.

By now Seymour Brolly and Septic – who had materialised from the front ranks of the crowd – were hemmed in to the gable wall and I said to myself Please Scotty, beam him up. I didn't want him beaten.

And yet he had been wrong, I was certain of it. A spit is so basic!

Septic pushed him in the chest. 'You slabbered over my dinner. Pig.'

He held on to his grip bag, both hands in front of his chest. Oh God, the binoculars, I realised! Were they really worth two hundred pounds?

'Didn't you? Pig.'

'No.'

He would fight, I knew. It would become inevitable. Yet he didn't look like a fighter unless he was a secret karate expert or something. Maybe he would do a Bruce Lee and Septic would fly through the air and land in a heap.

'You bloody well did. I'll slabber you!'

'It was my own dinner, leave me alone!'

Septic had reached forward, gathered a fist of shirt and tie at Seymour Brolly's throat and was now twisting, lifting, tightening, bringing him to the tips of his toes – when suddenly, in agony, Septic drew back, bellowing with rage and wringing his left hand as if to cool it down.

'He bit him!' cried Debbie.

Seymour Brolly tried to block the fists that now came his way with the grip bag, until this was knocked away and he was left with only his arms to defend himself. For a moment or two he tried to hit back and managed to turn Septic through half a circle by swinging on his tie: then the punches hit him in the face and he fell to the ground. There he lay, breathing heavily, looking up at his conqueror, winded and bewildered. Already the blood gushed from his nose. His eyes glistened. Tears, I think. The awful thing was, nobody went to help him up – I thought how if somebody gets hurt in the street people gather round and get blankets and make sympathetic noises, but such rules did not apply here. Seymour Brolly lay there and he was absolutely on his own.

And all for a bunch of whales scooting through the ocean blue, unaware that someone was giving blood for them behind the school canteen.

Eventually he crawled over to his bag and opened it and brought out his big glasses. After checking that they hadn't been broken in the fall, he zipped the bag shut and stood up.

He stared straight at Septic. 'The likes of you won't ever stop me,' he said.

Septic, scowling and unnaturally pale himself, hadn't a clue what that meant, precisely. As Seymour Brolly walked away the crowd split to let him through.

Debbie seemed well satisfied as we headed for the school buildings. 'Serves him right. Imagine spitting over your dinner, how disgusting can you get?'

I almost let the remark pass. 'It was his own dinner,' I said.

'And so? That's no excuse for wasting good food. There are starving children in Africa who would be glad of that jelly and I bet you a fiver it doesn't come from whales. How can you get jelly from a whale? A jellyfish, maybe. Who ever heard of a jellywhale?'

'Septic might be a big child,' I argued, taking a deep

breath, 'but he's not starving and he doesn't come from Africa.'

'Huh.' I was fixed on the end of one of Debbie's bayonet-like stares. 'You'll be fancying him next.'

. Fortunately we met Jill Neill, who looked totally miserable. Her favourite pop group had just split up and she needed sympathy.

Chapter

3

I finished *Under the Greenwood Tree* up in my room.

After hating it for the first forty pages I set it down wishing there was more, not wanting to let go of the quaint bunch of characters. I had been drawn unwillingly into the complications of their lives, and I was so pleased when Dick Dewey married his Fancy Day in the spring and they drove off together in a hay cart, down a lane, in the moonlight, to start their honeymoon. People can say what they like; a happy ending is a good thing.

Now I had to write essays and character sketches and plot summaries until I was sick of them.

How would they get on together, I mused – would he be good to her, and would she tire of being a tranter's wife and flirt like mad with influential people? With a bit of a jolt I realised that they weren't real anyway, and that even if they were, they would all long since be in their graves.

My room faces west, so I had a clear view across a few hundred lovely, peaceful miles of my planet to where grey-blue clouds as big as Wales blocked out the setting sun. Splurges of red seeped through in places where the cloud was thin, and the underparts of the clouds were lit up with liquid reds and golden lights. Between here and there, among folds and wrinkles in the rolling fields, were hidden small woods and rivers and perhaps small towns. A long line of diminishing pylons marched into the distance, carrying to faraway people the power to get things done. Fancy Day and Dick Dewey never imagined a hoover or a hi-fi, not even in their dreams.

Directly behind our house the next row of Swiss Chalets was already three courses of brick above the ground, and beyond that yet another row was marked out with T-shaped sticks. Civilisation was gobbling up the countryside in the wake of the marching pylons, and even though I couldn't very well complain – since I was living in a gobbled-up bit – I was sorry that my view of the sunset would soon be blocked out.

At the far end of the building site somebody moved in the vicinity of the huge sandbank. The workers had long since gone home, so I reckoned that Seymour Brolly must be messing about at something or other. Why did he spend so much time down there? Didn't he get on well with his mother? (I was curious about her.) How was his bloody nose? Why did I feel like signing his petition to His Royal Highness the Emperor of Japan?

I went downstairs, dug out my welly boots and threw on a coat. It was necessary to speak to my folks, who like to be kept informed of my movements, bless them; it's like a mild form of house-arrest.

'I'm going out for a walk, okay?'

'On your own?'

'Not if I had a dog, Mother.'

'Monica!'

Some people like cheese and some people don't, I thought as my feet slopped through the puddles, it was simply a matter of taste and you couldn't explain it. Debbie didn't like Seymour Brolly for some reason and for some reason I did – it was a matter of taste. To

Debbie he was a screech of chalk on the blackboard, to me he was a quiet tinkle of alpine cowbells. Wonderful imagery, I thought. Eat your heart out, Thomas H.

Seymour Brolly was so caught up with his activities in the shadow of the sandbank that I was able to observe him for quite a while before he spotted me. Now I saw that he was building something rather large, and not all together safe. The basic structure consisted of a long line of empty barrels at two-metre intervals. Around, over and among the barrels he'd packed in all the rubbish you could possibly find on a building site of Swiss Chalets – I mean sheets of rusty tin, concrete blocks, half-bricks and broken slates and discarded planks. The whole arrangement was linked from end to end with strands of barbed wire and festooned with strips of roofing felt so that it resembled the frontier between two unfriendly countries.

Then, while pausing for breath, he glanced up and saw me. Perhaps the hairs on the back of his neck were psychic.

'Monica.'

'Okay, I give up. What is it – the Berlin Wall?'

He wiped his brow with a loose-flapping sleeve. 'If you like. It's not finished yet. This is only the first storey and I haven't got a whole lot of time. Could you roll up my sleeve, my hands are filthy.'

Possibly, I thought, he was expecting World War Three and this was his answer to the Big Bang. I slithered down and tucked up his sleeve. His lower lip was swollen.

'Thanks.'

'All in a day's work. How's your face? Better than it looked at lunch-time, you were a real mess.'

'It's all right. I've got one of those noses that bleeds easily, I might have to go into hospital and get it cauterised.'

'Sounds like a good laugh.'

'They take a hot needle and burn the ends of some blood vessels up your nose.'

'Like being soldered.'

Seymour Brolly grinned, and said, 'Something like that.'

'I'd like to sign your petition.'

Now he rolled another barrel along its bottom rim until it fitted neatly into its proper place in the grand scheme of things, and looked up.

'Martin Grey signed it. I think he was sorry for me because I got beat up. Is that how it is with you, too?'

I flushed a little. Why? 'I don't know. Does it matter to the whales? Maybe I want a peep through your binoculars. Where are they, by the way, you don't look dressed without them.'

'Over there on a nail. Mr Thornleigh signed it. I like him, he's a very fair man. I asked Miss Irons but she thought I was taking the mickey out of her.'

Idiot, I thought. Debbie was dead right, he really could be a daft duck sometimes. I set my foot on a huge ball of barbed wire while he unravelled it, loop after loop.

'Doesn't that wire belong to the builder?'

'Yes, but I need it.'

'That makes it okay, then. Steal away. I hope they never give you a job in my bank.'

He smiled, and grimaced. 'My lip hurts.'

Don't spit, I almost said. 'What do you think of school, then?'

'It's okay.'

Now he anchored a loose end of wire under a block, and he proceeded to wind the long strand in and out like a gardener threading a rambling rose through an arch. Then he started to speak to me in a very matter-of-fact voice, as if talking into a tape-recorder, or something.

'I don't make friends easily. Some people can but I don't know how, there's a knack to it. Maybe we haven't stayed long enough in the one place, maybe it's the things I talk about. You need to know about ordinary things, like last night's TV. I'm quite intelligent, they think I'm a snob but I'm not a snob. At my last school I memorised all the teams in the four divisions of the Football League so that I could talk about football but it didn't help much. Maybe it's the way you're born.'

He stopped working to look directly at me. 'I'd like you to be my friend. I think you're a very level sort of person, very nice, and you can still call me Spacer like the others, I don't mind.'

You could have knocked me down, as Debbie would say, with a feather off a duck's behind. What did 'friend' mean, I asked myself?

'Why me? Is it my good looks or my charming personality?'

'Yes.' He laughed unexpectedly. 'Here, let me show you something.'

What next? I was ready for anything up to and including plastic mistletoe: but no, I was finally to get a look through the famous binoculars. They were surprisingly heavy as I pointed them where he indicated.

'Look at the sandbank just beyond the barrier and you'll see them.'

'You mean those birds?'

'Sandmartins.'

Dusk was beginning to close in, but even at this time of evening lots of nippy little birds zoomed in and out of holes in the red wall of sand.

'Isn't it strange how they never miss their hole? Like darts, really. Why are they so frantic?'

'The young have hatched, you see. They're quite early. It'll be a while yet before they can fly.'

I looked again. Zoom and ping – right in. They never missed. 'How far into the bank are the nests?'

'Longer than your arm. A metre.'

Bunch of proper little miners, I thought. 'It must be like a honeycomb in there. How come you know so much about birds?'

'My Dad bought me the field glasses when I was eleven and I've been interested since then.'

'Are they really worth two hundred pounds?'

'They're worth more.'

I lowered the glasses gingerly and returned them saying, 'I have to go or Mother will be out looking for me by torchlight. But thanks, that was interesting – really. See you tomorrow, probably.'

'Probably. I'd walk up the road with you, but I have to make preparations.'

For what, I wondered once more.

On the trek back home through the living-rooms of Swiss Chalets-to-be I started thinking about what Seymour Brolly had meant by the word 'friend'. He hadn't meant girlfriend, had he – mutual, exclusive devotion? Or did he mean I was to be a political sort of friend, an ally to be counted on in a world of hostiles? That, I decided, must be it.

But I knew he liked me, and the thought was flattering. And why not? Let's face it, Monica, everybody likes to be liked. He'd taken an awful chance, though. What if I'd responded with, 'No thank you, Spacer, I have too many friends already and in any case I like my friends to be popular and have prestige, all of which obviously rules out a wimp like you.'

Personally I would never have taken a chance with such a question, I don't like to be zonked.

Mother said, when I walked in the door, 'Have a nice walk, dear?'

'I saw some sandmartins, Mummy.'

'Well that's very nice for you, love.'

I didn't see Seymour Brolly in school next day because we didn't have an English seminar and he also failed to show up at dinner.

'See the effect you have on people, Septic?' Debbie said in Geography. 'You put them off their food. Typical.'

'Wasn't my fault. I wouldn't have hit him so hard only he tried to eat me, didn't he? Bloody cannibal. Look at that.' He produced a thumb for inspection. 'Those teeth marks are the real thing, you know.'

Debbie took his hand and stroked it gently. 'There, there, there my poor sick pet,' and Septic beamed like Number One Chimp being groomed.

Farleys, meanwhile, had been thinking deeply. 'We had fish today, right?'

'Brilliant, Farleys. Dinner was half an hour ago, how do you remember things?'

'No, listen. Would Spacer eat fish or is he just a friend of whales. Would he eat . . . cow . . . for instance?'

'He's probably one of those daft onions who only eat things if they're green.'

'They're called vegetarians,' I said.

'Oh lah-dee-dah,' said Debbie in her put-you-down voice. 'Anyone for carrots!'

I had no wish to get locked into a childish argument with Debbie, who has an inexhaustible supply of catty remarks at her disposal. Instead, displaying my talent for snide maturity, I let something slip as we were going to Home Economics.

'Martin Grey has signed Spacer's petition, by the way.'

'Oh?'

'Hmm. Yesterday. It seems he is on the side of the blue whale.'

'Lucky old blue whale,' said Debbie gloomily.

I was late home from school that day because I went into town to buy myself shoes. This is something I insist on doing for myself: Mother's taste is for brogues for the broad road and mine is not; but I have lived with the threat of bunions for long enough. Our phone was ringing as I came through the kitchen door.

'It's for you, Monica. Thingummy from across the road.'

'Never heard of him, Mummy.'

'Why doesn't he *walk*? It's from there to here, for heavens sakes.'

'It's okay, Mum, Daddy has shares in British Telecom,' I said, and she flashed me a funny look.

'Sometimes I wonder about you, Monica.'

That makes two of us, I thought, picking up the phone. He said, 'Hi. It's only me.'

'Hello, only you.'

'That is to say, I'm Seymour Brolly.'

'I know, I'm Monica Blake. Phone chats can be tricky at the start, can't they?'

'Well,' he continued after a pause, 'further to what you were saying last night . . .' (I wondered was he reading from a script) '. . . I have The Scroll ready for your signature if you'd like to call over.'

'You sound like a bank manager.'

'Do I?'

'I'll be right over, cage the alligators.'

His laugh was a deep and almost tuneful chuckle. I nipped out the back door while Mother was inspecting my new shoes – giving them two out of ten for sensibleness, no doubt.

The Brolly porch and the Brolly hall were a jolly green jungle of trailing vines, climbing creepers and monster

72

plants with brutal spikes and leathery leaves – altogether more impressive than your average rubber plant. The parrot among the foliage was a paper cut-out on a wire coat-hanger.

'The vulture's cousin, I presume,' I said lightly. 'Nice plants. Somebody sure has green fingers.'

'High humidity,' he replied.

'That would certainly explain it,' I said.

The Brolly living-room was the same shape as ours and there the resemblance stopped. The ceiling was painted in rippling circles, for all the world as if the light bulb had been a pebble dropped into a pond of soft colours. I had never seen anything like it. The Blake ceilings have always been white. Half a dozen paintings hung in the alcoves on either side of the chimney breast – studies in reds and yellows, each lit by its own strip-light. The red in the paintings was very red and the yellow wasn't mellow. The furniture was probably antique, though personally I prefer the word 'ancient'. They had a gramophone with an ear trumpet in the corner where we keep our hi-fi and their coffee table was an old Singer sewing machine. Clay objects sat about the place in various stages of construction or repair.

And I wondered: was this truly a Swiss Chalet?

'I hope you didn't mind my phone call.'

'No,' I said, fingering a clay bust on the Singer sewing machine. It had creepy blank eyes. No eyes, really. 'Who's he? Julius Caesar?'

Seymour Brolly pardoned my ignorance with a lovely gentle smile. 'My Mum's a sculptor. She's asleep in the bath right now.'

No bed, I thought? My brain-graphics popped up a vision of Mrs Brolly in the bath with blankets.

'Isn't she afraid of drowning?'

'Oh Mum doesn't drown. Her books get wet, though.

She reads, you see, and gets sleepy. Her hand drops and the book floats. She ruins quite a lot of books that way. The Scroll is over here.'

I followed him, thinking how I was dying to meet Mrs Brolly. The differences between her and Mrs Blake were of the black versus white variety.

'Yours will be the one hundred and twenty-first signature.'

Lucky old me. The celebrated document, now officially designated The Scroll, boasted three full columns of names. It was easy to see where the first-formers had signed while guzzling cheese and onion crisps. I made out the names of heavyweights like Mr Thornleigh (Christian name James), and Mrs Riley, who teaches Biology. The last entry said Thomas McAuley, Clerk of Works.

'Who is he?'

'The man who controls the building site. He was very obliging. I've asked him to stop levelling the sandbank until the young birds have left the nests.'

'And will he?'

'I dunno, he just laughed. If he sends in the diggers I'll just have to stop them.'

The truth, when it hit me, was a kind of mental clout. Here, then, was the reason for all that messing about down in the hollow. I saw it all – Seymour Brolly, dressed in khaki, preparing to take on an army of bulldozers, diggers, dumpers and bricklayers.

'So that's what it's all about! You're trying to save those birds, aren't you – that's what the crazy Berlin Wall is for!'

He straightened out The Scroll, pinned it down with a couple of clay owls and looked at me steadily.

'It's not the Berlin Wall and I'm not crazy.'

'Okay, you're not crazy.'

74

'Suppose you are right, would you be prepared to help me?'

I didn't even think about it, it wasn't worth the brain-time. Fighting bulldozers to save a few birds! Did he want my poor mother's hair to turn white overnight? No thank you, Spacer, save the world's wildlife on your own.

'I'm sorry, but I don't think it's really me.'

He handed me a pen. 'There you go. Signing your name – that's easy.'

I said, 'Is it!' rather sharply. The tone of his voice had quite needled me. Taking the pen, and with no thought that it might be read by the top man in Japan, I stuck my name under Thomas McAuley, Clerk of Works. Seymour Brolly rolled up The Scroll and patted it gently into the tube.

'It's better this shape, I can send it like a newspaper. I think it's probably more impressive than just an ordinary envelope, don't you?'

'Who knows the mind of an Emperor,' I said. 'We were wondering about you in Biology today, Farleys wants to know whether you would eat cow.'

'Do sharks eat mermaids,' was the very odd reply.

'What is that supposed to mean – do sharks eat mermaids?'

'It means that Farleys has little to wonder about if that's the height of his curiosity. You can tell him Yes, I eat meat.'

'So you're not trying to save all things bright and beautiful, then. You're prepared to see poor old cows butchered because you like a big steak but you won't let Septic eat blue whale?'

'The difference is that domestic animals are reared for food. I don't think we should destroy the last few animals of a species when we don't have to. Suppose the Loch Ness Monster turned out to be the last of the plesiosaurus, say – there'd be a worldwide outcry if some idiot shot it just for the thrill of having it stuffed, wouldn't there?'

'Certainly there would,' I said. Actually I wasn't sure.

'Okay. Someday soon somebody will fish the last blue whale out of the sea and people won't even know it. Monica, I do not mind eating meat – sailors used to take giant tortoises on board ship and eat them and that's fine, they had to survive. But I don't think the tortoises should be eaten nowadays because there aren't many left.'

'Personally I couldn't face a tortoise sandwich to save my life.'

'You'd be surprised, people eat practically anything. Think of four-and-twenty blackbirds baked in a pie.'

'People don't eat blackbirds!'

'People eat anything. They eat sandmartins. The birds winter in Africa and then they come north. It's a gauntlet, millions of birds come through the Mediterranean region and people know they're coming.'

'They shoot them?'

'Nets, traps, bird lime, guns, you name it. They cut the birds out of the sky as surely as they harvest corn – nine million birds a year. That's a lot of barbeques.'

I didn't speak. I hardly had time – there was more. 'Things wouldn't be so bad if it wasn't for the other problem. The Sahara desert is moving.' (I had a pop-up of camels towing a vast carpet of sand.) 'The desert gets bigger and there's more drought, you see. Only seven sandmartins reach this country for every hundred that came twenty years ago, and it might be less.'

By this time he had presented me with an open book from a shelf. It took me ten seconds to read a set of instructions on how to properly cook guinea-pigs and I do not tell a lie.

'They eat guinea-pigs!'

'They probably make very good hamburgers.'

Oh jeepers, I used to have one as a pet. I was heartbroken when I found it stiff one morning and dear old Dad thought it was good for me to learn about death.

'Seymour,' I said, 'the concept of a guinea-pig hamburger fails to turn me on.'

'I like to make you smile,' he said quietly. 'It makes me feel good.'

I wasn't even aware that I'd been smiling. He embarrassed me. Just when I thought I'd been teasing him about eating cow he pulled a switch, the conversation turned serious – and I wasn't ready for it. A warm flush came over my face and I thought how a blush is the most sneaky thing our bodies do to us, there is no rhyme or reason to it.

This explains why I suddenly developed a fresh interest in the clay Julius Caesar on the table.

'Who's is the baked head? You didn't say before whether it's meant to be anyone in particular.'

'It's my father.'

Oh God, congratulations Monica, one more foot put well and truly in it. I elected to say nothing. Seymour Brolly brushed the head with a knuckle.

'Mum did it when they were happy. It's actually quite like him. She kept him packed away in straw for a long time but I got him out when we moved to this house.'

Doesn't she mind, I wondered edgily. The man had walked out on her, after all. Does she ever feel like busting the bust, does she ever dust the bust with a feather duster?

I gave myself a mental shake and changed the subject as if I had never referred to his father as Julius Caesar. But how the devil was I to know!

'Have you done your essay on *Under the Greenwood Tree*? It's for Monday, don't forget. I like it, do you?

77

Well, I did after the first lot of pages, it gets better the more you get into it. I was just thinking yesterday how they didn't have all the machines in those days, but life was just as complicated, really.'

This speech of mine took us through the greenery and past the parrot to the front door.

'Mum's reading it,' he said. 'Poor old Dick and Fancy are probably drowning in the bath right now.'

We were laughing together when Debbie walked by with her dog.

'Hi there,' she said without pausing, '*very* cosy.'

I could cheerfully have strangled her.

PART

3

Chapter

1

'Saw you coming out of Spacer's house on Saturday night, Monica.'

I know you did, Debbie, I thought, I saw you seeing me, I was right there.

'Oh? Oh, yes,' I said.

'Showing you the alligators in his back garden again, was he? I hope you took a snake-fork, things run up your leg in the jungle.'

No, but I met Julius Caesar and a parrot, I was thinking. There isn't much you can do when Debbie gets stuck in the groove except wait it out.

'Of course if the invisible snakes don't nab you,' she went on, 'there's always the bottomless pit of quicksand, not to mention the vulture made out of cornflake packets.'

'He has an over-active imagination,' I said wearily.

'Imagination, is that what you call it? I mean to say, a cardboard *vulture* – what does his mother think when she hangs out the washing?'

'Debbie,' I said, 'we all pretend some of the time.'

'I don't pretend. Not since I was a kid, anyway.'

'Okay, you don't pretend.' I was heating up with each passing second. 'Everybody's not like you, people like to pretend, they have imagination – right?'

'No, it's not right. There's imagination and there's

pretending and there's loopy people who hand out snake-forks to total strangers.'

'Why don't you just stop this, Debbie?' I'd heard enough. 'Of course Seymour Brolly hasn't got snakes and blooming alligators in his back garden, nobody has, we all know that. But then neither do dolls have real hearts nor toy cars have real engines and all our teddy bears are full of just stuffing and foam. Paintings on a canvas aren't real, are they? Or the ornaments on a window-sill or that baldy head of William Shakespeare in the hall and *Under the Greenwood Tree* is only a book full of pages!'

'Monica . . .'

'I haven't finished talking yet, Debbie. You told Jill her hair was lovely when we know it's a mess. Yesterday isn't real either, it only exists inside your head and you wouldn't remember a thing about it if you were a panda in the zoo, it's part of your imagination and so is tomorrow. If you wiped out everything that isn't really really real on TV you'd be left with the nine o'clock news so doesn't life really call for a lot of imagination when you really really think about it?'

To be fair, I couldn't blame Debbie for gawking. She'd never heard my sweet lips spout forth pearls of wisdom in her life. I didn't sound much like the real me, even to myself. Miss Blunt was taking me over! But I stared back, just daring her to tell me to suck eggs.

All she did was shrug. 'Did you slip on a banana skin, honey?'

'No, I did not slip on a banana skin.'

'That's all right, then. What were you talking about, you and Spacer, if you weren't borrowing sugar.'

'I signed his petition and asked him did he eat cow.'

'And does he eat cow?'

'Yes, he eats cow. His mother's a sculptor and his father's . . .'

'His father's what?'

'I don't know. My mother says that the father walked out on them and hasn't been seen since.'

'Tough. He probably took a look at how Seymour was turning out and decided to call it a day.'

Maybe she was trying to be funny, I don't know – I'm only sure that she put the skids under what remained of my patience. 'Sometimes, Debbie,' I said, 'you can be one catty bitch.'

'Can I!' She was quite peeved, I could tell. 'Okay, Monica, be like that if you want to.'

If her walk was anything to go by as she stormed off, I needed a new friend.

A well-wrapped Miss Irons strolled into the courtyard and pirouetted slowly on one of her sensible low heels. With the brass hand-bell under her arm she looked a dead ringer for a town crier. An outrageous breeze dared to play with the ends of her chiffon scarf, causing it to flutter at the throat as she paced the courtyard like one of Nature's traffic wardens, making sure that pupils did not exceed the speed limit. One mustn't run in the courtyard, it is against the rules to risk bashing into some other person and breaking all one's bones. Some teachers can enforce the law and some can't, or can't be bothered: Miss Irons is one of those who can, and does. You just know to look at her that she is wound-up and ready to be totally destructive to anyone at any moment of the day or night, like a Cruise missile. That person might be you, so you don't step out of line.

Then a body appeared who was not exactly running, but definitely going from A to B at something more than walking pace. I think, actually, that Seymour Brolly had spotted me on my own and was on his way over – and though Miss Irons didn't know him from Adam the First, she immediately recognised the binoculars.

'You!'

At least one hundred people froze. When Miss Irons yells YOU it doesn't occur to her listeners that she might mean somebody else.

'You were running. Why were you running?'

How do you answer a question like that? You're doomed no matter what you say. Seymour Brolly tried to exercise some charm by saying, 'I must admit that I think I did break into a little bit of a trot.'

'Trot!' It didn't work, Miss Irons was not charmed. 'Only horses trot. What are those goggle things round your neck, are they growing there?'

'These are my field glasses, Miss.'

'And that is precisely where they belong – in the fields. Why do you bring them into school, what can you possibly want to look at?'

Poor Spacer, I believe he thought she was really interested.

'Different things, Miss Irons. Quite a lot happens even within the school perimeter, you'd be surprised. There's a pair of ring doves nesting on top of a telephone pole over there to the north-east, it may be unique.'

The glasses were offered, and declined.

'Listen, boy, the only thing that's unique round here is you. Individuals are all very well in their proper place, and this is not the proper place, is that understood?'

'Yes, indeed, Miss Irons.'

'You will not run in the playground. And do not bring binoculars to school.'

'May I please ask why, Miss Irons?'

'Because I say so!'

Anyone else would have let the matter rest there, but not Seymour Brolly, Citizen of the Milky Way. He was frowning politely.

'Are you sure that the rules of the school mention binoculars specifically, Miss Irons?'

People beside me gasped audibly. Among my fellow spectators – a rapidly growing group – were Septic and Farleys. Shut up, Seymour Brolly, I thought, desperately trying to silence him by mental telepathy. By now, though, I was beginning to get an idea of how he worked between the ears and I understood that he couldn't shut up. He wasn't being cheeky, merely asking for clarification on a point of law. But he didn't seem to realise, Miss Irons *was* the Law.

'You see, Miss, I was allowed to bring them to my last school. I think they took the view that my glasses were an educational device.'

I saw Septic nudge Farleys and purse his lips in a silent whistle of delight. His day was well and truly made.

'Were you!' declared Miss Irons, as she plucked the offending binoculars from around the offending neck. 'Then you simply have to be taught that this is a very different establishment from your previous school – don't you?'

Away she went, binoculars and all, busily flexing the arm with which she would shortly ring the bell. She barked out an order at an unfortunate first-former and sent him scurrying after a piece of litter that dared to blow past her nose.

I couldn't figure out, at first, what had come over Seymour Brolly. Shock, possibly. He held himself so very still, arms dangling loosely as if someone had switched him off. Water filled his eyes without quite spilling over into tears. Septic, always ready with words of comfort, muttered out of the side of his mouth, 'Hard luck, Spacer, it's bye-bye super-specs.'

'Miss Irons!' The call rang out with surprising force.

He held up two small black discs, one in each hand. 'Would you put these caps over my lenses, please?'

'I will do no such thing,' shouted Miss Irons, who now launched herself into ringing the bell lustily for the end of break. Perhaps it was my imagination, but her dings and dongs appeared to pack more decibels than usual.

Naturally, after ten relentless years of conditioning, we all moved smartly into line – except for Seymour Brolly. Like some stricken animal that could no longer move of its own accord he remained rooted to the spot until Martin Grey took his elbow and steered him safely into line.

I thought it was nice of Martin Grey to do that. Debbie had good taste in that department, at least.

That was on Monday.

Tuesday went by, then Wednesday, and still there was no sign that Seymour Brolly would get his binoculars back. It was the burning issue of the day – and I mean every day – especially Thursday's English seminar. Septic became politically conscious and turned militant.

'Spacer needs those peepers to look through, doesn't he? Right. Take my football boots. I need them to play football. How would I feel if she took my football boots, would I like it?'

'No,' said Faithful Farleys.

'You don't wear football boots round your neck, Septic,' Debbie pointed out, 'they go on your feet.'

'I might have them hung round my neck by the laces. I'm telling you I wouldn't like it so how can you say that's fair, eh?'

He sat back and surveyed the enthralled company, including Mr Thornleigh, who felt moved to draw

Septic's attention to the obvious. 'As I recall Robert, you took the glasses yourself only a few weeks ago.'

'Ah come on, Sir!' Septic was affronted. 'That was only a small joke between mates, wasn't it, Spacer?'

Even Spacer himself grinned a little. Then Martin Grey chipped in. 'Sir, it doesn't mention binoculars in the school rules, I've looked. Suppose I brought my snooker cue to school, or my electric guitar. Could she confiscate them, too?'

'Well . . . not in normal circumstances – why would she?' Mr Thornleigh looked uncomfortable, poor dear. 'But it's an unwritten rule that people don't bring valuable toys or possessions to school. They might get stolen. They *do* get stolen, and parents get angry. Miss Irons may feel that the field glasses fall into that category of things, so there it is. Now come on, out with the books. Talking is often educational, but sometimes a bit of work is required as well.'

Since my friendship with Debbie was still in a state of suspended animation, so to speak, I walked home by myself that day. It was a change to walk on the cracks between the paving stones without hearing dire warnings of disaster in my ear. At the end of Plantation Avenue I heard the bell of a bike ringing, and a voice called out my name.

It was Seymour Brolly, tie askew.

'Oh. Hiya, Spacer,' I sang out in reply. He slowed down, looked as though he might stop, gave a Lovely-weather-we're-having sort of a grin, and rode on.

Well done Monica, you gormless twit. Here is a person you like, who is interesting, is different, has an axolotl – who has an inexplicable interest in ordinary old you: and what do you do? You call him 'Spacer'. And how do you know he doesn't suffer from internal bleeding every time you call him Spacer?

I walked along the road saying Hello Seymour to

lamp-posts and How do you do, Seymour to other pieces of street furniture. Although I spoke out with great charm I had the good sense to stop before I got arrested.

Mother was weeding the front garden when I got home.

'Hello, pet, how was school?'

'Rather boring today, Mumsie.'

'Oh good. Monica, your Daddy says he sterilised this soil first but he couldn't have, could he? Look at the weeds.'

My heart went out to her as she gazed at next door's grass in mournful desperation. 'And look at theirs. They haven't even got a dandelion, for goodness sake. What sort of a tree is that?'

The red gloves pointed to where a sapling had been stuck in half way along the common fence.

'Oh well, I suppose it doesn't matter, a tree is a tree. Monica, we're thinking of getting Raymond one of those chess machines for his birthday. Have you got a piece of paper with the name of some computer written down?'

'Yes.' The clever Dick. 'And I'm not too fussy about a dog, Mummy, any sort of spaniel will do.'

'Now Monica, I don't want any more talk about a dog. Put the kettle on, dear, and make us a nice cup of tea.'

I did no such thing. Let Gary Kasparov make the tea for a change, I thought, and went upstairs to read my latest batch of Miss Blunt letters.

Although this was my last week but one in the role of Miss Blunt, my post-bag was heavier than ever this week because of Seymour Brolly's glasses – although the first letter I read complained that I was really Mr Thornleigh in disguise and therefore a fraud.

I looked for one letter in particular.

Dear Miss Blunt,

About eyes and thighs. Who are you to tell me that eyes are nicer than thighs, your head's a balloon. But I let that pass. I am writing about a certain person who shall remain anonymous. The fat cow had better give Spacer back his peepers or I will start a petition with many names on it and this petition will be sent to my Member of Parliament in the British House of Commons at Westminster.

One who seeks justice,
I am,
Septic.

I nearly split along the seams, frankly. They laugh most gloriously who laugh alone – if that's not a proverb it ought to be. Amid erupting guffaws and wheezes I longed to take the letter across the road and show Seymour Brolly that he now had friends in high places.

'Monica,' Mother called from the bottom of the stairs, 'are you all right up there?'

'I'm just having a laugh, Mother.'

'Couldn't you possibly laugh like a lady? The people next door will be wondering, dear.'

One cannot have the neighbours wondering, so naturally I restrained myself to another mild titter or two. In any case you can't just leave down a good laugh and take it up again like knitting a cardigan, so I was already in a more sober frame of mind when I read this:

To monica

Had I the heavens' embroidered cloths,
Enrought with golden and silver light,
The blue and the dim and the dark cloths
Of night and light and the half light,

I would spread the cloths under your feet:
But I, being poor, have only my dreams;
I have spread my dreams under your feet;
Tread softly because you read on my dreams.

I looked for a signature on both sides of the page but
there wasn't one. I read the lines over and over again
and they sounded lovely – like a bouquet of words,
somehow. But who was sending this to me? The only
certainty in my mind was that it could not be Septic –
that particular gentleman is no poet and he knows it.
For some awful, thrilling moment I even suspected Mr
James Thornleigh himself. My mind ran away into
newspaper headlines like TEACHER AND PUPIL IN
LOVE DUO and imagined he had left his wife and kids
for me and that people pointed me out in the street and
cried, 'Jezebel!'

Who else, then? Who knew, or had guessed? Debbie
would be up to it, of course, but she didn't have the
class for words like those. I have seen the verses on her
Valentine cards and they are basically a disgrace to the
English language.

I went to the window and saw that there was no view
at all through there, a soft mizzle had come in from the
west and filled in everything. The heavens' embroidered cloths were now a dull, wet grey. There was no
way I wanted that poem to be somebody's idea of a
joke.

Of course I know what love is, Mum and Dad adore
me like mad, I'm a chip off their old block, they own
me, I'm their gene bank for posterity. But what was it
like to be cherished by some random soul in the world
at large?

My heart was beating, it felt so *loud*. The neighbours
will be wondering, Monica, I thought.

Chapter

2

Then, at the beginning of a new week, the incredible happened. No horoscope throughout the land could have predicted what was about to happen to Miss Irons.

At break-time she took up her usual bell-ringing position on the courtyard step. The mere sight of her was enough to send most of us scrambling for the sanctuary of a straight line. To round up the few stragglers Miss Irons lifted the bell from its customary position behind the door and gave it a good ring.

She gave it a real good shake. But no sound came out. The bell was empty. It had lost its tongue. There was no dinger inside her to ring her.

I tried hard not to smile in case the wrath of Miss Irons should descend upon the meek and innocent. One set of my mouth muscles tried to force my lips sideways while another set held my mouth shut, the struggle was nothing less than heroic. Miss Irons turned the bell upside-down, glared into it, and began to rave.

'This bell does not *work*, someone has been *at* it! This is absolutely outrageous.' Her laser-beam eyes settled on a girl in the front row. 'Do you think this is funny, Madam?'

'No, Miss Irons,' the poor girl lied.

'Then go and find the Principal and tell him to come to the middle playground immediately.'

'Yes, Miss Irons.'

We waited patiently in serried ranks for the appearance of Napoleon, which is the pet name of our Headmaster. Septic, by now over the moon, whispered, 'This is magic, we've missed ten minutes of *parlez-vous français* already. *Oo la laaa.*'

The Head arrived, and now there were two heads peering into the empty bell, deepening the mystery. We listened for developments.

'The school bell has been tampered with. The inside has been detached and taken away, those are the facts. Miss Irons assures me that this must have been done during break, while the bell was sitting here, since it was intact at the beginning of break. Does anyone have any information?'

Heads turned sideways, anxious to miss none of the action. Not a soul broke ranks.

'It is my experience that this sort of thing cannot be hidden – the truth will come out. It is best to own up now, before a lie becomes inevitable, and then another. Well?'

The same grand silence filled the courtyard, and no one stirred. The Head finished, 'If anyone has any information, come to my office, please. That is all.' And the troops began to move.

We had an English seminar for the last forty-five minutes of the day. There may have been some sort of powwow among the staff, for Mr Thornleigh didn't arrive immediately. So Septic occupied the master's chair with an expression on his face like a born intellectual.

'Attention, you cloth-eared clots – the English language has been abolished. But first, I am about to read a dirty bit from *Under the Greenwood Tree* by what's-'isname. I will expect discussion. Ahem.'

'Give over you drunk duck,' said Debbie in derisory mood. 'What did you do with the school bell?'

'The bells, the bells!' cried Septic, *a la* Quasimodo. 'Esmeralda.'

'I bet it was you, Septic,' Debbie persisted.

'No. Ask Spacer, he's your man.'

Glory be, I thought, could he be right? Debbie spun in her seat to find Seymour Brolly hunched over his books.

'Did you, Spacer?'

'Did I what?'

'Muck about with the bell?'

'Mind your own business.'

'Suck eggs!'

Septic rattled the table and glowered imperiously at his class. 'Now. I shall read. This passage is dedicated to the lovely Sarah. I warn you that my voice will sound husky.' And it was. Very husky. '"Look at this lovely Fancy! Through the whole past evening she has been touchable, squeezable – even kissable! For whole half hours I have held her so close to me that not a sheet of paper could have slipped between us; and I could feel her heart . . ."'

Here ended the reading, for Mr Thornleigh came into the room at last, causing Septic to rise up as if he'd sat on a wasp at a picnic.

'Very nice, Glover.'

'Thanks, Sir.'

'You haven't read two consecutive pages of that book, yet you have managed to find a juicy bit. How? Explain, please. Why can Robert Glovers everywhere always find the juicy bit?'

'Easy, Sir – the geezer who had it last year underlined it in red.'

Even Mr Thornleigh threw back his head and roared out loud. It was a nice moment, I'm sure we had a good class after that, although I wasn't entirely plugged-in once it hit me that maybe Septic had got it right for a change. What if Seymour Brolly had zapped the school bell! At some stage I decided to wait for him at home time to find out the truth – and if necessary, to give him a lesson or two on the facts of school life.

First, though, I had to dodge Debbie, who wanted to walk home with me. We were on speaking terms once more since the dramatic events of lunch-time. Her news was that she was taking up snooker since Martin Grey had a cue.

In order to get away I simply told her that I hadn't a key and had to run home before Mum left the house to play squash. It came as an interesting shock that I could tell such a beautiful lie so easily.

I had a creak in my neck making sure that Seymour didn't whizz by on his bike.

'Hey, Seymour,' I called, feeling such a hearty fool, 'can I talk to you a minute?'

On went the brakes, up rose the front wheel and off slid Seymour Brolly while the bike was practically vertical. A display of virility, I guess.

'Very impressive, do you feed it oats?'

'It's not easy doing that, you know.'

'I'm sure it's not,' I said soothingly. 'It looks difficult. It looks practically impossible, really.'

I got a funny look for my pains. Now, I thought, was a suitable time to ask about that poem which had come into my life. It had struck me that perhaps Seymour Brolly knew something about those cloths of heaven. Pray, good Sir, what do these cloths represent, actually, why do you want to spread them out under *my* feet in particular; why should I tread softly, what are these dreams of yours that I'm walking on – do they involve me, and in what way, and what exactly is the big idea, anyway?

I didn't dare mention the cloths of heaven. In the first place I was afraid of being wrong – many a dog barks up the wrong tree – and besides, I suddenly thought of Raymond. My brother was surely the natural suspect, he might well have seen my Miss Blunt letters lying about and devised this latest piece of subtle torture.

Even more terrifying was the thought that I was right, and he *had* sent it. 'Yes, Monica, it was me. You are at the core of my every dream.' Good glory, I would die in the street there and then. I wasn't ready for romance, I couldn't handle the pressure and Mother is right, Monica, you are still a little girl when the chips are down.

How amazing, I thought, that Seymour Brolly should be walking beside me, oblivious to my intense mental indigestion. He steered the bike with one hand on its saddle.

'Very obedient bike,' I observed.

'It takes years of dedicated practise to do this.'

'You sound like a circus apprentice.'

'Just sheer skill. Have a go if you like.'

'No thanks. I'm not very good with mechanical things. Speaking of which, how is your Early Warning System coming along?'

'Well, the sandmartins are still there, if that's what you mean.'

I took a step into his personal territory. 'You messed up the bell, didn't you? It was you, Septic is right.'

'Clever Septic.'

Three lamp-posts went by and he didn't say a word.

'Well? Did you or didn't you take its thingummy out? And don't say it's none of my business because I'm making it my business.'

He glanced at me, briefly. 'Why?'

'Because I'm Hercule Poirot in disguise, why do you think?'

'Miss Marple would be more appropriate.'

'Cut this out, Seymour Brolly. Answer my question, please.'

'The bell isn't damaged,' he said.

'It's got no dinger! In my book that's serious damage if you're a bell. What use is a dumb bell to anybody, they're supposed to make a *noise*.'

'The correct term is clapper.'

'Dinger, clapper, what does it matter? Look, I know she's got your binoculars, but this isn't the way to get them back. It just isn't. I've been at the place longer than you have and she'll get you thrown out, she really will.'

'People should be fair,' he said.

I raised my eyes to the heavens above. Well of course people should be fair, they should be kind and loving and put money in beggars' hats, but just take a look at how the world is divided up – didn't he ever watch Dallas!

'You talk like somebody who's just graduated from Sunday School. Miss Irons is a fact of life. She's like one of those rocks that sailors stick a light on so they can sail away from it. You just learn to stay away from her. Most likely everybody who knows her stays away from her and she's the loneliest old witch in the whole world. Go to her tomorrow and grovel – please, Seymour.'

'Why?'

'I've just told you why.'

'No, I mean why are you saying this to me?'

'I'm supposed to be your friend, remember? I care what happens to you. Well, anybody, really. I don't like to see people in trouble, I'm training to be a Saint when I grow up.'

I got stared at: I mean so direct a stare that you can't tell whether the person is seeing you or seeing through you. Incredibly, his eyes misted over. Without knowing or sharing what he was feeling I watched him feel it.

'My Daddy gave me those glasses. I'm telling you, she'd better not scratch the lenses.'

Now, having spat out these words, he jumped on his bike and zoomed round the corner. We were within yodelling distance of the Swiss Chalets, so I guessed he would be home in ten seconds flat. For the first time in my life I wondered whether Miss Irons might not have bitten off more than she could chew – or at any rate, swallow. There had been steel in his voice. He had a cutting edge too, maybe. I had a fantastic premonition that Seymour Brolly was about to phone Napoleon and arrange a swap at dawn: the school bell clapper-dinger for two hundred pounds worth of binoculars.

Mother's hair was damp when I got in and she looked whacked.

'You have been playing squash again, Mummy.'

'Yes, Monica, I have been playing squash again. And so what?'

'Nothing. I'm not saying a word.'

From time to time I read her horror-snippets from the papers about what happens to squash players who are pushing forty. She knows that I would much prefer her to take up swimming, which is easier on the heart.

'I don't play to win, you know, Monica. I don't give my all, it's only a game. How do you expect me to get my exercise – pushing a hoover?'

'And weeding the lawn. Is that how you met Daddy? Playing squash?'

'No, I met him on a train.' She gave the most girlish little giggle I have heard from her in years.

'On a *train*?'

'Yes. What's wrong with a train?'

I had a black-and-white pop-up of the pair of them sitting opposite one another on the eight-o-nine, Father ogling Mother's legs where they disappeared up a mini skirt. Even before they exchanged two words I was probably a twinkle in my Daddy's eye.

'You mean you allowed yourself to be picked-up by a stranger on a train?'

'You read too many books, Monica. We went into town on the same train every morning, I hardly noticed your father.'

'And . . . ?'

'And what?'

'And something brought you together. The train crashed!'

'The train did no such thing. One day your Daddy objected to someone smoking a pipe in our non-smoking compartment so I backed him up and next day he let me read his newspaper on the train.'

'Wonderful. Sheer Mills and Boon,' I said, and Mother laughed like a hen quietly laying an egg – not at all like a lady.

'It was one of those decent newspapers. I remember I couldn't find the TV programmes and I crumpled all the pages trying to turn them. And of course, one thing led to another.'

'What do you mean?' I asked breathlessly. 'One thing led to another?'

'We went ice-skating.'

'Gee whizz big fizz, Mummy!'

'I liked ice-skating, Monica.'

'It's cold, damp and slippery. Did he ever send you poetry?'

'Who?'

'Dad!'

'Don't be ridiculous, Monica. But he once bought me a Rod Stewart LP. I can't for the life of me think why, that man is hoarse. And why are you so curious about such things all of a sudden?'

'Every girl is curious about her origins, Mummy,' I said, sweeping up from the table. 'It's only natural, *c'est la vie.*'

She swiped at me with the tea-towel as I went out.

Upstairs, I got to thinking about the Great Compulsion that comes over people to find themselves a partner. Dick Dewey sees the unforgettable Fancy Day at a window; Mother and Father are thrown together by the fight against air-pollution; dear Debbie is inexplicably crazy about middle-of-the-road Martin Grey. Funny, I thought, how the magic starts.

Chapter

3

Early the following week, as usual, I brought my Miss Blunt letters and replies to Mr Thornleigh so that he could take a look at them. This was the public end of the exercise – the things actually went up on the notice-board and my peers read them avidly – so I guess it was natural that he should check them over in case anyone went into a flap after the fashion of my mother.

The experiment, he said, had been a real success. 'Some of the writing has been of a very high quality. You've done well, Monica, I knew you would. And you've enjoyed it, too.'

'You didn't tell anybody it was me, did you, Mr Thornleigh?'

'No, they haven't a clue who it is. Why?'

'Oh . . . nothing.'

He clearly wasn't aware that he had had an affair with me and that we'd made the daily papers. His head began to shake as he read the letters and I saw his smile large and very wide.

'Fascinating. I see that Robert has discovered a cause worth dying for. The mind boggles slightly. I think it's probably best if we skip any reference to recent events, Monica.'

He meant, Ditch the binoculars correspondence – eighty per cent of my week's mail. 'I don't see why,

Sir.' I swallowed grimly. 'People feel very strongly about Seymour Brolly's glasses and they think that Miss Irons has not been fair. What is the sense of having freedom of speech only when it suits?'

My head was light with the effort of all this. It wasn't meant to sound cheeky and I hoped like mad that he wouldn't go through me. I meant it, though.

'A school is not a democracy, Monica,' he replied evenly. 'Indeed, one cannot get an institution further removed from the democratic ideal than a school, which is a hierarchy with many layers of power from the very top to the whims of the playground bully. The news-sheet is not about free speech. It's an exercise in the use of language, and that's all it is. Miss Irons and myself are colleagues.'

Blood is thicker than water, I heard myself thinking. 'What about Seymour Brolly, then?'

'What about him?'

'Those glasses mean an awful lot to him, Sir. His dad bought them and he's since gone away.' I hesitated, wondering should I go on. 'Can I tell you something in confidence, Mr Thornleigh?'

'You can. If you think you should, Monica.'

'Well then. He took the inside of the bell. The clapper bit.'

His face remained inscrutable. I had to go on, force a reaction.

'It was tit-for-tat, you see. He doesn't seem to understand what you can do and what you can't and he'll soon be found out. In fact I think he probably wants to be found out and it wouldn't surprise me if he told people himself.'

Mr Thornleigh continued to stare at me while slowly tapping the tips of his fingers together. Then he suddenly reached into a drawer and set a paperweight on the table beside us.

'In some ways I admire Brolly. He's one of those people who have their antennae up. But I have my reservations about him, too.'

The paperweight, I suddenly realised, wasn't a paperweight at all.

'Is that it? The dinger?'

'That is it. He brought it in this morning and expressed his feelings powerfully. I have seen Miss Irons and I think you'll find that Brolly has his glasses back quite soon.'

'But . . . what did she *say*?' I cried. Curiosity is a terrible force.

'As a rule, Monica, people are a lot more complicated than mere reputation gives them credit for. As a matter of fact she had no idea they were so expensive and had forgotten that the things were stuck away on the top shelf of her cupboard. Besides,' finished Mr T., steering me towards the door, 'I think she realises that in Mr Brolly we have something of an individual. Wouldn't you agree?'

I got stuck with a blush again.

PART

4

Chapter

1

How bang on the button you can sometimes be, Monica
– it really is funny, the way the magic can start. One day
coming home from school I sat for an hour and a half in a
bus shelter thinking about nothing but Seymour Brolly. I
don't know what I was feeling but it didn't feel like
happiness. Confusion, I guess. I had never thought for
so long a time about any other human being except
myself (I'm obsessed by myself, but then who isn't?), so I
knew that a rare old wind was blowing from somewhere.

Who was he anyway, I asked myself? Here was a
peculiar character with a fondness for animals and who
was inordinately attached to a pair of field glasses. Quite
probably he wasn't tuned in to what life was all about and
was never likely to be so. He had silenced a school bell,
didn't play football but knew the names of forty thousand
teams, was a frog who tried to join a choir of linnets,
corresponded with Emperors, and had bled for blue
whales. What a record! His poor wife, if ever he found
one, would spend her days searching for dinosaur bones
or the last gorilla in Borneo. He was off the rails.

Or had he learned, very early, something I could not
faithfully describe because I hadn't a clue what it was,
yet? His horizons were wide, his interest lay beyond
the moment and the merely personal – as Mr Thornleigh
had said, his antennae were up and every now and

then something in his head went bleep-bleep-bleep. His mind, I thought, was probably more enlarged than mine. Well, it would have to be, wouldn't it, Monica, to accommodate blue whales and a colony of sandmartins. I really did like him.

Someone was watching me. The handle of a tennis racquet stuck out from her sporty new green bag.

'Well well well, if I don't see Monica Blake sitting all on her ownio!'

'Hi, Debbie.' You fool, Monica, to be caught alone in a blooming bus shelter. I felt compromised. 'I expect you wonder what I'm doing here?'

'No, dear heart, I am not surprised, not a bit. That is typical Pisces, they like to sit and dream while life zooms by – not like us Gemini people, we like to get-up-and-go-buzz. How do you like the new games bag?'

'Very snazzy. A bit small for a snooker cue.'

'Granted. I've decided that nice girls don't play snooker, all that bending over is very rude. Tennis is the thing.'

'How's your game?'

'Awful – I'm still serving underarm. The court was wet, mind you.'

'Were you playing with anyone interesting?'

'Not *that* interesting.' She pulled a face, and broke off to stare at a piece of graffiti. 'Look at that. Isn't it the real truth!'

A bus shelter wit had written boldly BOYS WILL BE BOYS BUT GIRLS WILL BE WOMEN. 'Come on, Monica, snap out of it. I'm so hungry I could eat our dog.'

I rose up and said, 'Buzz.'

'Speaking of dogs,' continued Debbie, 'any movement on the four-legged friend front?'

'Yes. They're getting Whizz-kid a chess computer.'

'The rotten meanies.'

'They think a dog would scuff up the grass.'

'Gawd!' said Debbie. 'Grass!' She made it sound like a four-letter word.

Mother had company when I finally arrived home. Mrs Brolly sat in our kitchen and the hand which had shaped a thousand masterpieces now held a dark cigarette. The kitchen was fuggy with smoke but Mother, bless her, had provided her guest with a saucer and the window was wide open.

'Monica, say Hello to Mrs Brolly.'

I said Hello.

'So this is Monica, how are you dear?'

'I'm very well thank you, Mrs Brolly.'

'Of course I feel I know you, Seymour has mentioned your name, he says you're intelligent.' She turned to mother after a pull on her cigarette. Smoke leaked out with her words. 'He's never been interested in girls, you know what boys are.'

'There's time enough,' Mother said gravely as she pushed the teapot in my direction. The tea was like treacle but I sipped it anyway, taking all in. Mrs Brolly's wispy black hair was held in place by a red headband which perfectly matched her lipstick. Her eyebrows, like Seymour's, were like fine, dark feathers. Her body, lost in folds of multi-coloured cloth, was given a little shape by a gold belt at the waist. Good grief, I thought, maybe he'd meant it and they were all gypsies with a travelling circus.

I listened. Seymour had been a breech birth. I, Monica, had been put in the same bed as my sick cousin when we were both seven so that I could catch his German measles. Mr Brolly and Seymour had once helped toads across the road and she wouldn't open the door to him now if he crawled up the front path on his knees. The price of tomatoes, I heard, was beyond their understanding and so were the bin-men who refused to put the lids back on the bins. Mrs Brolly had once modelled nude for a pound an hour and she had bought her headband in the War on Want – Mother was scandalised, I could tell. I felt like the original fly on the wall, this was riveting stuff. At one point I pictured Mrs Brolly in the bath, reading, then slipping under the water to drown without knowing it. They would come and lift out her stiff body, dressed only in a negligee of soapy bubbles.

There were three broken butts in the saucer when Mrs Brolly stood up. 'Well I must fly, mustn't I? Seymour eats like a shire horse in this weather, one couldn't fill him. Do call over for a chat, Helen, and it was super meeting you, Monica. 'Bye.'

Mother was left in the middle of the kitchen with a pair of rather rounded eyes, which she turned on me. This was it, I thought – Mrs Brolly was about to be summed up in one bombshell of an opinion.

But no. 'Well, she's rather arty, isn't she?' Mother said mildly. This seemed to remind her somehow of smoke, for she suddenly began to waft the window to and fro. I left her to it.

About an hour or so later I was looking for sellotape in the sideboard drawer when I realised that my photograph was missing.

Actually, it was my best photograph. I wouldn't have minded had it been one of those school efforts in which I have freckles on my face and hair like a rope. In this photo I wasn't Miss United Kingdom, exactly, but I had a bit of style and a bit of shape and my shoes had a bit of a heel. Where, I wondered, had he hidden it? After looking behind the sideboard and under the flap of the carpet I made a bee-line for the kitchen, to where Mum had been banished. Sport was on in the living-room and she had to make-do with the portable TV.

'Mummy, my photo has gone from the sideboard.'

'Gone where, love?'

'I don't know but it had better be found for I am

getting *sick* of this, he turns me upside-down all over the house and now he's made me disappear altogether.'

Mother groaned and marched forthwith to the door. 'Raymond! Come in here immediately.'

IT made one of his more careful entrances, all sweetness and light. He was too much the expert at pushing people to the limit not to realise that this was possibly trouble.

'Right. This photograph business is going to stop once and for all. Where is it?'

'Where's what, Mum?'

'Monica's photograph from the sideboard, get it right now, bring it here.'

'Okay, will do. Can you give me a couple of days, Mum, I hired it out to one of the boys in school.'

My poor mum was reduced to staring at her own son as if he were an alien. 'You hired it out?' she echoed weakly.

'Only for a pound, Mum, I can easily get it back, no harm done.'

No harm done, he said, and walked away scot free. Not so much as a tap on the behind or a clip round the head or a harsh word in his ear for making money out of facsimilies of his sister! The crime was so outrageous that Mother was thrown off balance – there was no precedent, it was outside her experience, she was paralysed. 'Well just see that you do!' she called out when the schemer had gone.

Some time later I quietly entered his bedroom after knocking ever so politely. I was only about to throttle him. He was learning some Latin vocab. And playing the chess computer at the same time.

'Who's got my photograph?'

'Just business, Moan – no hard feelings.'

'Who did you give it to, you greedy shrimp!'

'Classified information.'

'Raymond, if someone is looking at a picture of me I

want to know who it is. For all I know Robert Glover is throwing darts at my face right now.'

'It might be Septic and it might not – I promised my client complete confidentiality.' He finished off this remark with an impersonation of Woody Woodpecker.

'Suit yourself.' I unplugged the European Chess Champion and dangled it in front of his eyes. 'Two can fight dirty. I'm going to hire this thing out for 50p a week until you change your mind and you'd better believe it because I am telling you that I don't feel good.'

'It was Seymour Brolly.'

Carefully I lowered the computer to the table once again. 'Seymour Brolly gave you a pound for my photograph?'

'Yip. But only for a week, that was our understanding. I didn't sell it to him because I knew you'd miss it.'

'Whose idea was it?' I asked, keeping it light. My blood was on the move, I could feel it in the rims of my ears.

'Possibly mine. He was always asking questions about you in chess club so I thought I'd do him a favour. Every time he looks at you he sees moonbeams, didn't you know? I could have got a fiver for a lock of your hair, no sweat, but it was too risky. You might have wakened up and seen me with the scissors and there might have been a misunderstanding.'

What a mercenary little beast, I thought – but only in passing. Some things were falling into shape. If he paid through the nose for my photograph then he must have sent the poem, too, there was no one else. I went back to my room in something of a tizzy and changed for bed.

Right now, at this moment, was I perched up on his dressing-table between the alarm clock and some piece of pottery, smiling down at his head on the pillow?

It was not easy for me to believe utterly that anyone could look at me and see moonbeams. I guess it felt like my heart was doing a wheelie.

110

Chapter

2

My mother patted her hair-do on Saturday morning while staring hard at Mirror, Mirror on the Wall, and cheerfully declared: 'Stars above would you look at me, I'm like the wreck of the Hesperus!' Then she sailed through the front door with the car keys in her hand.

She was happy. She would return in about five hours with aching calves and a bag full of brochures about bedroom suites. So long as there is a room to be furnished in the Swiss Chalet she will never be bored and the truth is that my father is just as obsessed with playing house. He agonised for months on end over what sort of fireplace we should have. 'Helen, dear, it's such an important focal point, the first thing they *see* is the fireplace!' And would Italian marble crack with the heat or would polished granite be better? We spent a fortune on it.

Mother wasn't gone five minutes before she was back again. The exhaust on our car has a kind of throaty growl combined with the tinkling of reindeer bells, you can't mistake it. As soon as Mother appeared through the door I knew something was wrong.

'Did your Father get up yet, Monica?'

'I've no idea, what's up?'

'It's that boy, Seymour Brolly.' And she raced up the stairs yelling, 'Frank!'

I was really mad with her for rushing past me like that and leaving me so anxious to *know* – as if I was a non-person. My first thought was that his body lay squashed under the wheel of some lorry at the end of our road and such a pulse of terror went through me that I shook. So I left the house running, and half-way down the hill I met Debbie coming up and she let out a shriek.

'Monica! I was coming to get you, you're missing it all. Spacer's finally flipped and they're going bananas down there. Hey wait, you daft duck, you're still in your slippers!'

Travelling, so to speak, as the crow flies, I careered madly up the glistening ridges and down the guttery gullies to where the sandbank loomed large against a fleet of dark clouds and I thought how this was it. Battle had commenced, the high-rise birdie flats were coming down, they blocked the way west.

All of a sudden I hit a new road, or at least, the beginnings of a road. Already that morning they had laid down a broad highway of grey, clean stone. Where this track ended two monster lorries were parked with their angled backs directed towards the planets. The driver of a yellow JCB smoked a cigarette in the privacy of his cab. I noticed that the glass had been cracked in some previous encounter. The jaws of this machine hung in mid-air, waiting for orders. Three workmen sat outside a hut, sharing tea from the lid of a flask. One of them glanced over at me, and winked.

'Saucy sod,' said a voice behind. Debbie had caught up with me. 'Monica, he's stopped all the work. There's one guy in green wellies and he's fit to be tied, you should hear the language he's coming out with. What is Spacer playing at, the green bean?'

There was an audience already. Groups of local people had gathered on convenient platforms of cement

112

blocks to observe the fun. I scrambled up a freshly made mound of topsoil, and saw him.

Seymour Brolly was down there in the shadow of the sandbank. The assorted items of building site debris, assiduously collected over the weeks, had now taken on the shape of a huge, arching structure which strangely resembled a bizarre work of art. Under the central arch of this thing Seymour Brolly sat hugging his knees. Of all the details I noticed about the weird scene, one seemed more marvellous than the rest: the birds continued to fly in and out of their nests, like darts hitting targets, as if none of this fuss concerned them. Ignorance is bliss, I thought.

'Those barrels look wobbly to me,' said Debbie. 'Do they look wobbly to you? I wouldn't sit under that lot for a pension.'

Yes, Debbie, they look wobbly to me. I wondered if he saw me. A lorry arrived, a third snorting monster like the other two, full of stones so clean they might have been made at a factory. The driver shouted from his cab, 'What am I going to do with this lot? Will I drop it here?'

'No!'

It was the man in green wellies. His neat check cap and expensive fawn overcoat seemed to put him a cut above the other workies as he turned to the person at his side. 'That swine is sitting down there like the man on the bloody moon. Get him out. I don't care how you do it, just get the idiot up here!'

Debbie dug me in the ribs, and hissed. 'What did I tell you?'

'He won't come up,' said the other man. Was this Thomas McAuley, I wondered, Clerk of Works? 'He says he's there for the day, sandwiches and all.'

'Sandwiches?'

'He's got a packed-lunch.'

113

'Well, I'll be damned! That is rich, that is really rich. You've got a dozen or more men on this site and none of you can go down there and haul the fool up by the short and curlies. Eh?'

. His face filled with blood, giving the colour that was redder than your average blush. This was shortening his life, I could tell.

'Look,' said the Clerk of Works, 'I'm paid to prepare a site and that's what I've done. If you want him up, you go down and get him up. But I'm warning you, he's handcuffed himself in and if that bloody great wall of China comes down they might as well dig the both of you out with *that*.' He jabbed a finger at the high metal jaws of Godzilla the JCB, and walked away.

For the first time I noticed Mrs Brolly. Dressed in an anorak and headscarf, she leaned on a pile of roof tiles like a refugee from some war. I scrambled over to her.

'Mrs Brolly, are you all right?'

'No. If I had six pink gins I still wouldn't be all right.' She flapped her arms hopelessly. 'This is getting out of hand, don't you see? It's getting out of *hand*.'

It occurred to me that maybe she had put Seymour up to this stunt, the whole thing was her idea, maybe that arrangement of junk down there was her idea of Art in Action. 'Mrs Brolly, you'll have to get him to stop, he just can't do this.'

'Or they'll bury him,' added Debbie. She was referring to the third lorry, which still had not dropped its load of laundered hardcore.

'*Me* get him up? What can I do? He thinks he's right. I might as well talk to the clock on the wall. He made himself sandwiches this morning and said he was going out.' Suddenly she raced forward and grabbed Green Wellies by the arm. 'Please, he believes very strongly in what he's doing, can't you . . . I don't know. Can't you . . .'

114

'Lady, I've had enough of this bulling about. That JCB is starting to move and your boy had better shift his butt.'

The engine chugged into life. Godzilla gave a lurch and a clank and its shovel began to descend. The metal caterpillars had begun to crunch over the stone when, unaccountably, it conked out – an event which fetched a cheer from some spectators on their mini-hilltops.

'I filled it yesterday,' called the driver. 'He must have drained the tanks.'

'Well fill it up again!'

'You're the boss-man,' said the driver with a shrug.

Debbie jerked my sleeve and nodded over to her right, where music had started up. 'Look who has arrived with his tape of Golden Oldies.'

It was Septic and Farleys with some of their mates. The ghetto-blaster at their feet blared out Status Quo and 'Rockin' All Over the World.' All that was now required, I thought, was for a van to turn up and start selling hamburgers.

'Debbie, I'm going down to speak to him.'

'Spacer?'

'Yes! Spacer.'

'Gawd. You think you should?'

'I think somebody should.'

'Monica, my sweet fish – have you gone loopy about him?'

'Debbie, suck eggs.'

She was worried about me, bless her, I could tell by her frown. Probably the teletext horoscope for Saturday was warning all Pisces people to stay away from building sites.

What exactly are you going to say to him, Monica, I asked myself during my downward slither – and I hadn't the foggiest. 'You can't stop progress' seemed an appropriate line to take, but I knew he wouldn't

115

listen, his brain refused to decode such obvious messages.

I said 'Hi,' and he looked up like something hunted into a corner. You were a breech birth, I thought, and saw that sure enough, he was tied to the barrier by lengths of twine.

'Hi yourself. You should see your feet.'

'Never mind my feet, Seymour Brolly, I hope you know what you're doing down here because nobody else does. There's a man in green wellies up there and he's getting ready to send in a JCB after you. It's got teeth, I've seen them.'

'Let them. They wouldn't dare. They think I'm tied in.'

'And are you?'

'Do you think I'm stupid? It only looks that way. And they haven't the right.'

'But they have. They have the right. They paid their money, they bought the land, it's all theirs, sandmartins and all – they own it.'

'Not the birds.'

'They own the birds: the birds, the insects, the worms, the insects, everything, the blades of grass – they own it! And they've got the power. You can't stop them, Seymour, please come up.'

'I can't. They'll all die. They came five thousand miles to lay their eggs in this place.'

He gave me such a look that I got down on my knees and put my arms around him tight and rocked him like a baby – but I did these things within the total privacy of my imagination. How did one get to have such an affinity for sandmartins, would he ever love a person like that? Up on rock-and-roll hill our DJ Septic was playing 'Bat Out of Hell': heavy metal had arrived.

'I hear you're buying up old photos of people at inflated prices?'

'You know about that.'

'I know everything, where is it?'

'Between page fifty-one and page fifty-two of my Biology book.'

Gee whizz big fizz, I was stuck away face to face, probably, with the nervous system of a rat. Somebody called my name.

'Monica! Come up here this minute. Right now, and I mean it! Do you hear me?'

Father had arrived, arms flailing like a broken-down windmill. Daddy, I thought, you are a complication and a nuisance.

'You'd better go,' said Seymour

I went. Pater was not pleased with me. 'Are you mad? Monica? Look at your feet! Do you want to be killed?'

'No, Daddy.' This statement, though it was the truth, did not appear to improve his temper.

Meanwhile more spectators had arrived, like extras in a crowd scene. I saw Septic, now in his element, cup hands round his mouth to yell, 'Hey, Spacer, if you're still there at lunch-time we'll throw you a hot chinese!' When an enormous gust of laughter died down the tape had changed to Bruce Springsteen singing about his love for a Jersey girl.

'Oh Gawd listen,' cried Debbie, 'I just love that song!'

And over there Mrs Brolly was standing in the metal jaw of the yellow great Godzilla, right in, she's Boadicea, I thought. She shuddered with each chug and my daddy, who hates scenes, tried not to stare at her but he stared. He stared and the driver of the lorry picked his nose like some faintly puzzled, patient chimpanzee as Manfred Mann sang 'Pretty Flamingo' and umbrellas went up against the spitting rain and cows stared over a faraway hedge as only cows can stare. Zoo. One Christian and a yellow lion, circus and zoo. I sank on to a cement block and stupidly began to cry. I don't know why, or for whom, I felt as though I had been flattened by a great big rolling blob of absurdity.

It was nearly over, though. Green Wellies suddenly scampered along the track of stones with new life in his boots because a police car had just arrived. Things were different now. Septic switched off his music and silence rushed in to smother everything.

The young policemen were in no hurry. Perhaps, I thought, they are specially trained nowadays to move slowly and with dignity. Down the slope they marched and began to speak to Seymour Brolly.

In this way the whole thing ended. A uniform is mightier than a machine. They and he came up the slope together, and when they had reached level ground Robert Glover, who cannot abide silences, put his hands together in a solitary round of applause.

'Good try Spacer old son,' he called. 'Hang on in there.'

Seymour Brolly and his mother were taken away, whereupon Godzilla lurched down the slope with its jaws swinging and Seymour Brolly's barricade came down like a house of cards.

'She was inside the bucket! She was standing in the bucket. She was actually right inside the bucket of the JCB when the police arrived, wasn't she, Monica?'

Daddy had not yet recovered from the events of the morning. In spite of television and its many powerful images, he is still rather easily shocked.

'Yes, Daddy, she was right in.'

Mother didn't even bat the proverbial eyelid. I suspect she thought that if one buys ones clothes in the War on Want shop, one might as well stand in the bucket of a mechanical digger.

'It's a good job they came,' said Daddy. 'The site

contractor was beside himself – ready for action. Things could have turned very nasty.'

'If you ask me,' said Mother, 'she's really got her hands full with that boy. And she's on her own, too, which can't make it any easier. There are some children and you just can't do a thing with them.'

You've got one, I thought, his name's Raymond and he's sitting at the table right now, taking everything in with his big ears.

'I wouldn't like to see him in ten years time,' Daddy said grimly.

'Why not?' I asked.

'Well – just look at the way he gets on.'

'How does he get on?'

'I mean he's a fanatic. He'll grow up to be the sort who chain themselves to railway lines because they think they're right and the whole world's wrong. I'm not against people having their point of view, but there's a limit.'

'Are you sure,' I said quietly, 'that you have all the facts?'

'Hey, Mum – do we have to talk about this stuff?' Raymond asked suddenly. For once he was totally ignored.

'What facts?' asked Daddy, glaring at me as if all the facts in the world were his personal property.

'Seymour Brolly doesn't look at things the same way as you do.'

'Now you're talking. *That's* a fact.'

'He thinks that maybe there's another way of doing things so that we leave a little bit more and destroy a little bit less. What's so fanatical about that?'

'But Monica dear, people need houses,' said Mother.

'Not in the next fortnight!' I cried. 'Those birds would have flown in another few weeks.'

Mother sat back silenced. Not so Father.

'Those men down there are builders, and in case you don't know it, to a builder, time is money.'

'Ah for crying out loud,' sighed Raymond. Mother bullied him with a stare and Father went on, scarcely aware of the interruption.

'They have contracts to meet, their jobs depend on it, they can't afford to wait for birds to hatch. There's always a rabbit warren or a fox's den or a bird's nest where people build, and it's tough, and I don't see why you feel you have to defend this sort of behaviour, Monica.'

Mother said 'Frank' very quietly and I took in breath. There comes a time when you know you're about to hurt and get hurt.

'That's because you don't make the effort to understand how other people feel.'

'That's enough, Monica,' said Mother. There was a sudden clatter as Raymond set down his knife and fork.

'I don't want us to talk any more about this.'

'No, let's hear it!' Father said, almost in a whisper. 'That young fool disgraced himself and his mother, caused a neighbourhood scene and had to be led away by the police. Not to mention the cost! More than a dozen men and God knows how many machines idle for two or three hours. They should sue him. So what else is there to understand? And sit down when you're talking to me!'

'What do you care!' I was standing, I was screaming. 'What do you know about anything? What do you know about me? You know *nothing* about me, I should have been a bloody wordprocessor. Let them plough baldy blind birds into the earth and it won't worry you, all you care about is grass – grass and grass and *grass*.'

I took off with as much sense of direction as a headless chicken – it felt like any old place would do; except I turned down the hill rather than up in case I met Debbie and had to account for the state I was in. A car bumped along the road behind me and I felt sure it must be them coming after me. It wasn't, but to be safe I turned sharp left into the dusky depths of the building site. This was the first time their little worm had ever turned.

I was such a disappointment to myself. All the people I admire are cool and unflappable people who keep their feelings inside, out of sight; just now I'd turned myself inside-out and let them have a real good look at the brain and being of the real Monica Blake. I had lost my head – it went right out the window.

Stupid, Monica, stupid. How quickly a person can unravel, like a badly sewn seam.

Eventually I looked around and saw where I had wandered to. The bank which had been such a land-mark was no longer there, they had levelled it. Sharp stones crunched under my feet, those same, clean, factory-made stones I'd seen arrive that morning and which now seemed such a far cry from the cloths of heaven under my feet. I looked into pools of water where oil had spilled from the snorting monsters. Dark colours turned there like dying rainbows.

I didn't care about the birds, not at that moment, not really. They were under there somewhere – the baby ones, anyway. In my mind and in my being, Seymour Brolly had arrived. My miserable heart ached for his company.

That's when I heard the sound behind me, and it was scary. Nothing sobers me up like good old-fashioned fear and this site in the half-light seemed like the perfect place to wind up a crime statistic.

'Monica? Is that you, Moan?'

It was brother Raymond. 'No, I'm the Abominable Snowman. What do you want? I suppose they sent you to fetch me home?'

'They didn't send me. I came by myself.'

I was sorry. He was, after all, a fringe member of the human race. I said, 'How did you find me?'

'Luck. I didn't think you'd stop running. Moan, listen, they're really feeling black and blue. Mum's blaming Dad and he's not fighting back, now's your chance.'

'For what?'

'A dog. You come back with me now and I'll steer us all round to talking about it. Okay? Moan?'

Just when I thought I'd never laugh again, he almost sparked a giggle. Only my brother could think of blackmail at a time like this.

'Idiot,' I said. 'Come on.'

'I can do Mr Magoo,' he said as we walked. 'Would you like to hear my Mr Magoo?'

He did Mr Magoo. On the way I then had to suffer Pluto talking to Popeye and Popeye talking to Olive Oil and Olive Oil talking to both of them.

'Raymond.'

'What?'

'You owe Seymour Brolly one pound.'

'You're right. I'll give it to him on Monday when I get your picture back.'

'Don't bother, I'm giving it to him – free.'

Normality had returned by the time I got home – indeed, it seemed that normality had never gone away in the first place. Mum looked up and smiled as if I was fresh in from school and Daddy glanced over from the display of his share prices on Ceefax. He has five hundred and thinks he owns British Gas.

There was no way I could pretend. I had the feeling – maybe not the right feeling, I don't know – that things had shifted and the family would not be the same again: not exactly.

'I'm sorry for the scene,' I said. 'It was mostly my

fault. I'm never doing that again. From now on I'm staying to say what I have to say, I won't ever run out again.'

Precisely how they took that I didn't wait to see, I went straight to my bed, hoping against all the odds for a quick conk-out and pleasant dreams. Some days you just want to forget.

Chapter

3

I didn't see Seymour Brolly on Sunday – my guess is that his mother kept him in quarantine all day and probably fed him on bread and water. Until eleven o'clock when Raymond saw him open the front door and bring in the milk, it was possible to believe that he had been thrown in jail.

Debbie called by in the afternoon. Hadn't yesterday been a laugh, wasn't Spacer a daft duck, purple onion and green bean, and should she enter Collie for a dog show next month or would the scraggy mutt disgrace her? The scraggy mutt in question deposited a smelly parcel on our front path, which Debbie deftly flicked to one side with her foot.

'Makes the grass grow. See you in the morning, Monica.'

'Goodbye, Deborah.'

'Gawd I hate that name, I wish I'd been called Carmen. Come, Collie-wolly – walky-walkies!'

We gathered as usual on Monday afternoon for Mr Thornleigh's seminar, where Septic greeted Seymour Brolly as if he were a mobster out on parole.

'Hey, Spacer, did they give you a rough time in the clink.'

'They read me the Law of Trespass.'

Septic whistled, he was impressed. Then he noticed a cardboard tube sticking out of the grip bag.

'What's that? Is that a telescope?'

'Leave it alone.'

'Just a peep, Spacer, I want to look at Sarah, close-up.'

'It's not a telescope. It's my petition to Japan. I'm posting it today.'

Where, I wondered again, had he got the address? Septic raised a hand dramatically. 'Which one of my fans is going to lend me a pen? Sarah? Please?'

Sarah Topping quickly zipped-up her pencil-case. She had no intention of aiding and abetting the infidel. Debbie produced a biro with a dire warning.

'I want that back, Scumbucket, or I'll thump you.'

'Promise. Right, Spacer, get it out.'

'No. You'll tear it up.'

With his right hand on his chest, Septic spoke in hallowed tones. 'May the Big Chief up there strike me stone dead, Spacer, I'm not messing.'

Out came The Scroll, which was duly peeled open for Septic to sign with a flourish. 'There you go. This petition, with my name on it, will swing it for the blue whales. Their worries are over, Spacer.'

'Gawd!' said Debbie, wrestling back her pen. 'That is typical. Look what he's done, the goof, he's signed it "Septic". What are they going to think when they see that in Japan?'

If they ever read it, I thought darkly. Any one of a thousand Japanese civil servants could cheerfully twist it up and aim it at the nearest bamboo bin; the Emperor would never read the glorious name of Septic. Then Mr Thornleigh arrived and sickened us with talk of exams.

My next class was French and Seymour Brolly went off to the Silicon Chip Biology class, but there was time for a quick exchange in the corridor.

'How many names have you got?'

'Three hundred and sixty-nine – no, and seventy.' He

made it sound like millions. 'I'm sending it away this afternoon if you'd like to come to the Post Office. If you're free.'

'Well for Heaven's sake, how could I miss it?'

He smiled at me, and I felt like the element in a kettle when the power goes on. Like magic, really.

'I've got a crow to pick with you, Seymour Brolly.' I said in the street. We were on the way to the Post Office.

'I don't eat crow.'

'You wrote me that poem, didn't you? I mean the one that turned up in Miss Blunt's box.'

'No.'

I hit the panic button. Was there somebody else? Were two people looking at me and seeing moonbeams? Then I saw that he was blushing.

'You did so!'

'I didn't write it, I stole it from an Irish poet.'

'I hope he sues you.'

'He can't sue me, he's dead.'

Drowned, I mused, by his mother in the bath. 'How did you know it was me?'

'I didn't. Mr Thornleigh was behind the scheme and there aren't many people who could have been Miss Blunt. The religious girls are too narrow-minded, and the others are too stupid. It had to be you.'

Whizz-kid me, I thought. He went on, 'I didn't know you'd got it until now. Don't you like it?'

'When I work out what it means I'll let you know if I like it.'

We had almost arrived by this time at the Post Office. Sheer curiosity prompted me to lift the cardboard tube out of his bag and it was addressed to the Japanese Embassy in London.

'Cheat!' I cried. 'You told me you were sending this to the Emperor of Japan.'

'The Emperor is only a titular head. He doesn't make decisions. Here we are.'

I half expected some sort of scene inside the Post Office. But the clerk weighed it without even thinking that it might be a long bomb, then stamped it, and set it to one side for collection.

We came outside. 'Are you pleased,' I said, 'now that the blue whale is safe?' I took his hand to emphasise that this was basically a friendly remark.

'You still think I'm crazy, don't you?'

'Crazy but nice. I'm going to let you keep my photograph and I won't charge you rent if you promise to take me out of your Biology book.' I swallowed. 'Just quietly, I like you very much. I really do.'

'I like you very much.'

'Not as much as those sandmartins, I bet. And there's only one Monica Blake. I'll be extinct, soon. Jeepers, what a thought!'

'I like you better than sandmartins, blue whales or anything else on the face of the earth.'

I got the wobbles. Such words are commonplace, I am sure – they have been said before many times to many people: but never to Monica Blake. They were awesome and inexorable, I felt like the tide was coming in.

'Well. . . . What next, now that you and Septic have saved the whale? The great white shark?'

'Toads,' he said.

Glory be to heaven, all creatures great and small! 'Toads?'

'My Dad and I used to belong to a group who helped toads across the road. They get squashed by cars, it's a real problem.'

'Only if you're a toad,' I muttered. Inside my head

was a pop-up vision of a motorway black with warty big hoppers.

'I could easily,' he said, 'make you a TOAD CROSS-ING lollipop out of a round board and a plank. You'll enjoy it.'

Seymour Brolly suck eggs, I thought.